HANDS FASTER THAN LIGHTNING

THE BEGINNING

BRENT A. BOHN

Brent A. Bohn

Printed in the United States of America

ISBN (paperback): 9780578217277

eISBN: 9780578464039

Library of Congress Control Number: TXu 2-110-534

Cover and Illustrations by Rebecca Shaw
BrockleyDesigns.com

DEDICATION

This book is for my parents – Lucille and Richard Bohn, who endowed me with their love of the Old West and inspired me to compose this book.

My parents loved all types of western books; 1950s and 60s television series like *Gunsmoke, Bonanza, Lawman, Bat Masterson,* and *Have Gun, Will Travel;* and John Wayne movies including*: Stagecoach, Red River, She Wore a Yellow Ribbon, Sons of Katie Elder* and *True Grit.*

ACKNOWLEDGMENTS

First and foremost, I would like to thank my wonderful other half, Diana Gearhart, for editing the rather long-winded, poorly punctuated first draft of this novel. The grammar was so terrible that she quit after about sixty pages, announcing that if she wanted a job, she'd pick something else to do.

Throughout the writing process my good friend, Jim Gallahan, not only served as a great inspiration to me, but helped me explore countless plot twists and writing strategies over our many working lunches.

My gratitude goes to my sister for beta-reading and editing a later revision of the manuscript. Jerilyn is a avid reader of many genres and I respect her insights and opinions.

I am also grateful for the large body of published research about this era that provided me with the valuable historical data and statistics used in the novel.

I would also like to thank my editor, Carol Strubel-Krimm, for her tireless work and professionalism in clarifying my ideas and improving the flow of my manuscript.

Finally, many thanks to my graphic designer, Rebecca Shaw, for creating a beautiful cover and interior chapter designs for this novel.

About the Author – Brent Bohn

I was born and raised in northern Virginia and graduated with a B.S. in Business Management from George Mason University. After thirty-six years, I retired from Federal government service and now live in Warren County, Virginia.

Although I am an avid reader of fantasy, mystery, detective, adventure, sci-fi, horror and ghost stories; I have always particularly loved tales of the Old West. When I was a small child, westerns were the most popular programs on television and the superheroes of the day were lawmen.

Since then, a love of the West has always been a big part of my life and inspired me to write this series. In my search for period accuracy, I have travelled through ghost towns in Nevada and Texas and experienced the authentic feel of the wild west in Tombstone and Old Tucson, Arizona.

To learn more about this author and future publications, please see www.brentabohn.com or BaB_Books@twitter

TABLE OF CONTENTS

SHIPROCK, NEW MEXICO – 1883

Bill and Cody were about the same age, but as different as night and day. Bill happened to be the local bully, while Cody was the son of the town sheriff. Bill made life miserable for everyone who was smaller or weaker than himself but particularly disliked Cody, not only because Cody was the son of a lawman, but because his mother was a Native American.

Since they were young boys, Bill had taken every opportunity to harass Cody and his taunting had escalated to physical confrontations as they got older. Today's fight started when Cody was walking down the street with a small bag of candy and Bill ran over and smacked it out of his hand shouting, "It's high time you learn who's the real boss in Shiprock. I'm gonna' teach you a lesson you won't soon forget."

With that, Bill swung his right fist toward Cody's chin in front of the dry goods store. Cody blocked the punch with his left forearm and hit Bill squarely in the stomach with his right fist. Bill grunted as the air whooshed out of his lungs. Bill returned the favor by slamming Cody in the stomach. The boys grappled with each other and raised a large cloud of dust as they rolled around on Main Street, each trying to get in more punches.

Cody's father, Sheriff Richard Anderson, saw the ruckus and ran down the street to break it up. He had to pull Bill off Cody, as the heavier boy had gotten the upper hand. "You fellas stop fighting! What started this?" demanded the sheriff. Neither boy responded as they rose to their feet and looked stonily at one another. Sheriff Anderson ordered Bill to head home and kept a watchful eye on him as he stomped down the street. Cody paused to dust himself off and pick up his candy. His father then took him by the elbow and headed toward the jail.

"What's up with the two of you? It seems like you guys are always fighting."

"Bill is a jerk. He always picks on younger kids at school or those around our age he thinks he can whip. I'm just guessing, but I think he gets bullied by his brothers and picks on everyone else to blow off steam."

"Well, try and stay away from each other, hopefully before one of you gets hurt."

Cody agreed to try. Nothing else of interest happened the rest of the day.

It was early dawn on April 11th when Cody was awakened by his father. The air still had that chilly spring bite. April could be downright cold at times, in the 20s in the morning but a pleasant 70° by afternoon. In midsummer, however, the temperature could spike to well over 100°. This was desert-like country, mostly dirt, sand and sparse plant life. Shiprock only had about seven inches of rain a year.

What little drought-tolerant vegetation struggled to survive the brutal conditions included twelve different varieties of cactus, ranging from very large to small; desert bushes like ocotillo, jojobo bean, creosote and Indian tea; hardy agave and yucca plants; and the ever-present sage brush and tumbleweeds. The only trees in the area grew near the San Juan River, except for a small number of Joshua trees that seemed to pop up anywhere.

Cody's father stuck his head into his room and shouted, "Come on Cody, wake up! I need to get to the jail early today, so that I can let Clem out."

Cody wiped the sleep from his eyes as he sat up in bed. He remembered that last night his father said that they would try to go fishing in the late afternoon. Cody knew their chances were good, if no trouble cropped up in town today. They had a favorite fishing spot along the San Juan River, which wound around Shiprock from the north about half a mile to the east side of town.

Cody was very close to his father and loved to go fishing with him. They would sit by the river against a Utah Juniper with a quirky corkscrew trunk and talk for hours, poles propped over their knees, or just lay back on the sandy bank and watch the clouds go by.

As Cody came out of his room, he saw his father cooking eggs for breakfast with a few thick slices of bacon for each of them. There were also some biscuits that Mrs. Wilson had baked for them just last night. She and her husband John owned Shiprock's only hotel and restaurant.

Cody was sixteen, although he would emphatically declare that he was sixteen and a half. He was already five feet, eight inches tall and would most likely match his dad's six-foot two within the next few years. Cody weighed one hundred fifty pounds, had raven black hair, deep brown eyes and a square face with a prominent chin and a long thin nose. He also had long thin fingers (which would have been the envy of any concert pianist). Except for his cheekbones, he looked most like his mother Maria, a pretty Navajo woman who died a year earlier from cancer.

Cody developed his hard, muscular frame by working in the livery stable toting hay bales and lifting sacks of grain for the owner. For his hard work, Cody made three cents a day or twenty cents a week. He worked after school to help pay for food and clothes, as well as gratify his insatiable sweet tooth for candy and chocolate. Since the dry goods store rarely got any chocolate, Cody almost always had a piece of candy in his pocket. If it melted, Cody would try to pull off the sticky mass at the bottom and eat it anyway. Hopefully, wash day would remove the rest.

Cody and his dad lived in a small house on the eastern outskirts of Shiprock, New Mexico, close to "Four Corners" where the borders of Utah, Colorado, Arizona and New Mexico meet. Shiprock was on the trail used most frequently by groups of dreamers headed up from Arizona into Colorado after the Gold Rush began in 1859. There was always a steady stream of people moving through Shiprock. Freight wagons passed through twice weekly, and even the stagecoach came through town once a week.

Prospectors had found gold all over the Denver area – there were valuable strikes at Central City, Cherry and Clear Creek and along the South Platte River. In 1864, miners also discovered silver at Georgetown, just south of Denver. This brought even more people into the area, including folks who were down on their luck and looking to strike it rich relatively quickly.

For the most part, the local businesses around these mining towns were the only ones making loads of money, as supplies were in high demand. Every miner needed to buy picks, shovels, sifters and pans. The strikes also brought fast "guns for hire" in Colorado, not only to guard the shipments of gold and silver from the mines to the banks, but also to work as bodyguards for the mine owners.

There were sixty-five people living in Shiprock, with an additional thirty or so on local ranches in the area. Most of them were Navajo Indians. Richard had been sheriff for about five years now. Up to this point, he had never been in a gunfight with either the cowboys in from the trail or the local ranchers. That's not to say that he didn't know how to handle a gun. The sheriff could take care of most issues with a warning or his fists but wasn't afraid to use a firearm if it came down to it. About the only incidents that happened with any frequency were the drunken cowpokes that he had to put in jail for the night when they got too rowdy and started breaking up the town's only saloon.

Richard was raised on a Pennsylvania farm until he enlisted in the Union Army at age 18. He rose through the ranks to become a Calvary officer, where he used his pistol with regularity. Richard came West after the war and worked as a cowboy at one of the local ranches around Shiprock.

He had originally planned to go to California because of the Gold Rush, but he met Maria in town and never left. They had Cody shortly after they were married. A few years later, Richard took a job as deputy sheriff and succeeded Harry Robinson as sheriff after Harry retired. Sheriff Anderson had a pretty good draw, but it wouldn't hold up to some of the faster guns that rode the West.

Over the last few months, Richard had begun teaching his son how to use a handgun. The boy was still a poor shot and had not yet even attempted to draw a pistol from a holster. Cody had occasionally gone deer hunting with his father's rifle, so he was at least somewhat familiar with that weapon. Cody kept a twelve-inch Bowie knife in his right boot, purchased with his first pay from the livery stable. Cody had used his knife to skin a couple of white tail deer his father shot over the past year. His dad promised that he would teach Cody more of the basics of drawing and shooting a six-gun as soon as he got time, but Cody was impatient.

Some other boys his age had already been practicing and would tease him about his poor marksmanship. Cody told himself that the kidding really didn't mean much, but it was starting to get **real** old. He decided to ask his father for lessons once again after they got out to their favorite fishing hole today. Cody hoped that his dad would finally find the time one day soon to teach him more about drawing and shooting a gun.

The day began like any other Saturday. Cody was glad that he didn't have to attend school. He planned to do a half day's work at the livery stable before he and his dad went fishing. Cody always enjoyed these excursions. He could spend some quality time with his father without any distractions, and they would discuss all sorts of things.

Cody liked to listen to his father reminisce about his childhood and the place where he grew up. His dad had lots of stories about his adventures and different things that happened to him over the years. Cody was never quite sure if all these fantastic tales were true or if his dad was just pulling his leg.

Before Cody started work, he always changed into the overalls his father bought him a few months ago. He knew he had to muck out stalls and replace the straw and didn't want to get the mess on his shirt and pants. Cody didn't much care about getting dirt on the overalls because he knew they would be washed every month.

Cody figured no one would see him in his dirty overalls anyway, since Jeb Gordon, the owner and blacksmith, was the only one that met people coming into the livery stable for service. Usually, that involved fixing loose horseshoes or replacing lost ones. Occasionally, Jeb would board horses for people that were spending a few days in town. Less often, he repaired wheels or axles for buckboards and wagons.

After breakfast, Cody and his father washed the dishes and made their lunches, which consisted of ham sandwiches with mustard and a slice of cheese, an apple and two butter cookies from Mrs. Wilson. She was an excellent cook and made delicious meals and baked goods at the restaurant, so the place was always busy.

Cody's mother had been good friends with Emma Wilson. After her death, Mrs. Wilson tried to make sure that Cody and his father had some decent meals a couple of times a week. Occasionally, she even sent over a real treat in the form of an apple or cherry pie. Of course, such tasty tidbits didn't last too long around the Anderson house because both Cody and his dad loved their sweets.

Richard pinned his badge to the front of his shirt and then put on his gun belt. He never tied down the holster unless he knew there was really going to be a need for it, and there seldom was. Absentmindedly, he patted the smooth brown grip of his blue steel 1873 single-action Colt .45. This new gun replaced the old 1851 cap and ball Colt pistol he had used as a Calvary officer.

The sheriff had heard that some gunslingers were now beginning to mark their grips with one notch per kill and didn't particularly like this news. He felt that all life was important and shouldn't be reduced to notches on someone's gun.

The elder Anderson was already headed out the front door when he called out, "You'd better hurry up, son. I've got to get to the jail pretty quick."

"I'll be there in a second, dad. I haven't gotten on my other boot yet." As soon as he yanked on his boot, Cody shot out of the house and ran after his father, just remembering at the last second to lock the front door. By the time Cody reached his side, the sheriff was striding west down Main Street into town. Cody glanced down the street toward the outskirts of town and noticed some movement stirring up a big dust cloud a couple of miles away. "Look dad, someone seems to be in a hurry out west of town to make all that dust."

"Probably just some people that have been on the trail for a while and are happy to see civilization."

"Are we expecting a group in town from one of the local ranches?"

"Naw, not that I've heard about."

After walking for a few more minutes, the pair arrived at the livery stable. Before heading inside, Cody reminded his father about their plan, "Dad don't forget about going fishing this afternoon. I know you sometimes forget things once you get your head into those office books and wanted posters."

"Don't worry son, I won't forget. Just you remember our side bet on who's going to catch the biggest fish."

"Yeah, I'll remember, but it's you who'll be doing the dishes for a week because I'm going to win the bet."

"I don't think so, smarty! I can see myself now relaxing all week while reading a newspaper or book," chuckled his father. Cody waved goodbye and headed into the stable to find Jeb Gordon and get his chores for the day.

The sheriff walked a little further down the street toward the jail and stopped. He glanced out of town again toward where they first noticed the dust rising. He could just barely see the lead riders now.

Richard stepped up onto the wooden walkway in front of the jail and unlocked the door. He walked into the office and unhappily eyed the new wanted posters piled on his desk that he would have to read.

He hadn't received any notices for several weeks, until this stack came just yesterday on the stage. The weekly coach stopped for an hour or so to rest and water the horses. During this break, passengers and drivers had time to stretch their legs and get something to eat from the restaurant or buy a drink at the saloon.

The jail was not empty this morning because Clem, the town drunk, had spent the night in one of the cells. Richard pondered the unfortunate fact that this seemed to be happening more often lately.

Clem swept the saloon floors for money, most of which he handed back to Frank the bartender by the end of the day. Clem also tried to bum beers or shots of whiskey from the customers. He'd sit down and chat with any of the locals he could in the hope that they'd buy him a drink in return for some current gossip or news.

The sheriff shrugged off this train of thought as he hurried across the outer office and opened the door leading into the back and the two jail cells. He hollered but Clem didn't respond, so he yelled louder, "Clem, wake up!" as he opened the cell door.

"Stop yelling, I kin hear you. It's not helping my head any, you yelping like a coyote."

"I'm sure Mrs. Wilson will have some leftovers from breakfast that she is saving for you over at the restaurant."

"I wish she'd include some whiskey with breakfast instead of always pushin' milk on me."

"You know she's pretty much a teetotaler. Besides, she wants you to coat your stomach so that you don't get ulcers."

"Yeah, all the same, it's my stomach."

"Go on now. I don't need you hanging around here all day." The sheriff slowly closed the cell door as Clem, still a little tipsy, wobbled through the door separating the jail from the outer office. Weaving back and forth, Clem managed to get the outside door open and stumble into the street. As soon as he was alone, the sheriff came around the desk to sit down and begin his least favorite chore, scanning wanted posters.

The dust outside of town grew larger as the group of six riders approached. Rick Brenner, Alfredo Torrez, Dave Sjogren, Jorge Rangel, Jim Gallahan and Robert "Big Bob" Stevens were all wearing "dusters," knee length coats that would repel rain and keep the dust off their clothes.

Four of the men had cheap gray dusters. Big Bob and Jim were the only ones wearing the more expensive tan dusters with a thin fur-like inner lining that protected against the cold and could be removed in warmer weather.

These six men were not hombres to be toyed with. Jim and Big Bob were downright mean most of the time. Big Bob was the leader of these thugs, who billed themselves as "gunmen for hire." These desperados had left Tombstone,

Arizona well over a week ago and were tired
of being in the saddle under the blazing sun.
Tempers were getting frayed along the edges and,
if they didn't come across a town relatively soon,
things might erupt.

Rick and Alfredo were rustlers on the run
from the law around Tombstone. They weren't
averse to shooting a small ranch owner in the
back when he was out on his range and then
stealing his cattle. They figured they'd better get
out of Arizona for a while before someone strung
them up.

Rick stood five-foot nine, had an average build
and a slightly round face with light brown hair
that he kept short. He talked a lot and liked to
laugh. Rick rode toward Shiprock wearing a black
shirt, gray slacks and a tan cowboy hat.

He'd been raised in Illinois and always dreamed
of going West where he thought everything
was exciting and wild. Rick had stolen some of
the neighbors' chickens and hogs when he was
sixteen. They got the law after him, but he saw
them coming and escaped out the back door. Rick
headed West and never looked back.

Alfredo Torrez was about the same height
as Rick, but more slightly built. He was born in

Mexico and had brooding dark eyes, black hair, a goatee and a mustache. Today, he was wearing a white shirt, black pants and a faded black sombrero. He had a gold incisor tooth on the top right side of his mouth. The tooth and the two-inch scar on his left cheek were souvenirs of a long-ago knife fight in Los Reyes.

Alfredo's older brother was one of a group of banditos robbing travelers along the road. Alfredo soon followed in his brother's footsteps and joined the gang too. After his brother was killed during a robbery, Alfredo decided he would head up to New Mexico to try his hand at cattle rustling. Being rather quiet, he never talked much, except with his pal Rick.

Dave Sjogren stood five-foot ten with light brown hair and green eyes. As he rode toward town, Dave wore a white shirt, brown pants and a dirty brown Stetson. His father was a Swedish dry goods store owner in Mankato, Minnesota and his mother earned a few dollars a week washing laundry for the townspeople.

Early in his life, Dave worked as a bank teller but was fired and spent two weeks in jail because he "borrowed" five dollars from the cash box to take out his new girlfriend. When the girl discovered what he did, she dumped him.

Dave decided he needed a fresh start and headed West. He tried cow-poking around Tucson, Arizona, but it was hard, boring work that paid little money. Dave caught a break when he was hired as a shotgun guard for the stagecoach that ran between Tucson and Tombstone. He started hanging out and drinking with Jim and Big Bob at the Tombstone saloons.

Jorge began as a trooper in the South Dakota Badlands. He constantly got into trouble at the fort and hated taking orders from his superiors. He didn't stick around after being dishonorably discharged from the Army. Because he was an above-average poker player, Jorge then tried to make a life as a gambler. That ended when he killed a man in a Topeka, Kansas saloon who called him a cheater. Fortunately for Jorge, the dead man drew first, and the other players backed his claim of self-defense.

He moved on to Arizona and got hired as a poker dealer in Tombstone's Birdcage Saloon but was quickly fired after numerous customers caught him cheating. Jorge was a stocky five-foot nine with dark brown hair and eyes. His father was said to have been Cuban and his mother was from Iowa. As he headed toward Shiprock that April morning, Jorge wore a red shirt, black pants and his blue trooper's hat.

Jim and Big Bob had fought in the same Confederate unit during the Civil War. They had saved each other's lives several times and had become close friends. Jim was a small, wiry man with close-cropped dark hair and muddy brown eyes who stood only five feet, seven inches tall. His battered cowboy hat matched the dull gray of his shirt and pants as he rode toward Shiprock.

At six-foot four, Big Bob towered over his friend and was, by far, the more dangerous of the two. He was a massive man with black hair and piercing brown eyes, weighing in at over two hundred fifty pounds. As was his custom, Big Bob was dressed all in black from his Stetson to his boots.

Besides his duster, Big Bob's only visible extravagance was a solid silver belt buckle engraved with the threatening face of a long horn bull. Some of the mine owners in Tombstone wore these buckles to display their power, and he liked the look. Both Big Bob and Jim wore spurs with long sharp rowels, unconcerned about the bloody

31

flanks of their mounts. Unlike most westerners, they didn't care about their horses.

Both gunmen had quick tempers and didn't take crap from anyone. After they mustered out of the Rebel army, their first order of business was to hunt down the officer in charge of their unit. They thought he was incompetent and blamed him for nearly getting them killed several times during the war, so they broke both his legs and almost beat him to death.

Jim and Big Bob were both good shots and had mastered the art of fast-draw shooting while robbing banks in Texas and Oklahoma. Eventually, they decided to head further West to get out of the reach of local lawmen. To make money, they hired themselves out to whoever needed fast guns. Most jobs netted at least a couple hundred dollars. Of course, the longer the job, the more money they charged.

Big Bob and Jim had just finished some guard work for one of the silver mines down in Tombstone. But when the mine started to play out, they were let go and needed to find other work. They read about new strikes in Colorado in the *Tombstone Epitaph* and decided to go there. Months earlier, they had run into Rick and Alfredo in Tombstone while drinking and playing poker at a local saloon.

"Hey, Big Bob, how long do you think it will take us to get to Denver?" asked Jim as they rode.

"Somewhere close to three weeks, I reckon."

"We've been on the trail for nine days already and my butt's getting saddle sore."

"Oh, stop yer bellyaching. Maybe we can spend a few hours in the next town, so that we can stretch our legs a spell. Hopefully, there'll be a good place to eat and a fully stocked saloon with high quality booze."

"I hope they have better whiskey than the last place we hit. It was so watered down, I thought we were drinking sarsaparilla."

"There's just no pleasing you, is there?"

"Sure. Just give me a willing buxom gal and some good whiskey and I purr like a kitten," laughed Jim.

It was almost 9:30 in the morning when the weary travelers entered the town limits. The men could see that Shiprock was like a lot of other little settlements dotting the sparse western landscape. There were several adobe houses on either side of the trail at the beginning of town, another row of houses behind these and various larger buildings with houses interspersed between them laid out from west to east near the center.

On the left side of the street the men first noticed a saloon and a dry goods store. A little further down they spotted the jail and Wilson's Hotel and Restaurant at the far end of the street. On the right stood a gun shop and, further down, a livery stable and blacksmith. The men were just passing the first few houses when Big Bob spied the gunsmith's shop.

"Jim, you take the others over to the saloon for some drinks. I want to visit the gunsmith to get my trigger loosened. I can get some extra bullets while I'm at it."

"Okay Big Bob. While you're there, pick me up a box of rifle cartridges." Jim and the others turned left and tied their horses on the rails by the front doors of the saloon. Big Bob turned right and tied his horse in front of the gun shop.

"I'll be glad to get some of this trail dust out of my throat. I nearly choked to death the last few days," Jorge whined.

"I wish you had. It would have saved us from eating your breakfast this morning," replied Dave.

"Haw! Haw! Very funny. Just for that, you can take my turn from now on," Jorge bellowed.

Pushing open the swinging saloon doors, they stepped inside and could see only one person besides the bartender. It was Clem, who appeared to be passed out at the first table in front. The five gunmen moved between the first few tables and bellied up to the bar.

"Hey, barkeep! How about some drinks?" hollered Jorge, slapping the bar. Frank hurried down the bar toward the customers from where he had been cleaning and polishing some glasses.

"What can I get you?"

"I'll take a shot of tequila."

"Me, too," added Alfredo.

As he poured the tequila, Frank announced mechanically, "That'll be two bits from each of you."

Dave and Rick ordered and received shots of the house whiskey before Frank looked questioningly at Jim.

"Bring a bottle of your best whiskey and two shot glasses over there," Jim ordered, pointing to the table closest to the back wall. He strolled over and sat down facing the front door. This way he could see anyone entering the saloon. He always sat facing the door, so that he could see the law or any other potential trouble coming.

The gun shop was a small adobe structure that stood some distance from the other buildings in town in case of an accidental fire or explosion. Gunpowder is awfully touchy at the best of times. If the store caught fire, at least it wouldn't bring down the whole town with it. The building had a dirt floor instead of the usual wooden planks. This was also by design to keep down potential fire hazards. The shop door had a cow bell that would clang when it was opened. That way, the gunsmith could hear potential customers arrive if he was working in the back.

Big Bob strode up to the front door and opened it. He entered a room about ten feet long by eight feet wide with two display cases running down the right side. Inside these cases were two dozen different handguns, several Derringers and some Bowie knives.

Against the wall behind the display cases was a tall, locked gun cabinet containing several rifles and shotguns. No one was in the front when Big Bob came in, so he went over to one of the displays to see what was available. As he bent over to peer into the case, he heard footsteps approach from the back room.

"Can I interest you in a new sidearm?" someone asked.

Big Bob looked up and turned slightly to see a tall lanky fellow in his late fifties.

"I'm Tom Haines, the gunsmith. What can I do for you?"

"I need to loosen the trigger on my pistol. For some reason, it's been getting harder to pull lately and I like a real hair trigger response. I also need a box of .45 bullets and cartridges for a Winchester 30/30."

The gunsmith saw that his customer was a big burly guy with a scowl on his face and noted that he wore a single holster slung low on his right hip, the hallmark of a gunslinger. Right off, Tom knew that it would be wise to be very cautious around this man.

"I can certainly do that for you. It'll take about a half hour to fix your pistol, depending on the problem. If you leave it with me, you can return in a little while and pick it up then. So, how many boxes of shells do you need and what was the caliber of your pistol again?"

"I need two boxes of bullets for my .45 and you might as well give me two boxes for the 30/30. Oh, by the way, I am in a little bit of a hurry so make it snappy on the repair. I don't like to be kept waiting," Big Bob declared with a wicked grin. He bought the ammunition, then walked out of the shop toward the saloon.

The gunsmith thought to himself, '*I don't like this new customer and I'm going to warn the sheriff about him as soon as I'm done repairing this pistol.*' Shiprock had not seen too many of these real hard cases in a long time, and he was glad about that. Tom hadn't seen Richard this morning, but he knew the sheriff was probably already at the jail by now.

Tom picked up the gun and went toward the back room to start working on the trigger mechanism. The sooner he could fix this pistol, the sooner this guy and anyone else he might have brought with him would get out of town. Tom had been to other big towns over the years and had seen his share of some of the biggest baddest gunman.

This guy seemed to fit the description. He knew gunslingers usually ran with a bunch just like them. '*Maybe there are others of his kind in town right now.*' The thought gave Tom a very uncomfortable feeling that he just couldn't shake.

Big Bob led his horse across the street, tied it to the hitching post by the saloon doors, entered the building, made his way back to the table where Jim was seated and sat down. Jim slid him a glass and passed Big Bob the bottle of whiskey.

"Did you get my cartridges?"

"Yeah. I didn't want to tote all those boxes around, so I put them in my saddlebag for now. You can pick them up on the way out of the saloon. If you are in an all-fired hurry, you can go get 'em now yourself," Big Bob replied sarcastically.

"Naw, it can wait. How long is it going to take to fix your gun?"

"About a half an hour. That gives us some time to drink, so let's get started before we have to leave this hick town."

"I hear what you're saying. This fly on a cow's ass place reminds me of where I grew up. I couldn't wait to leave it, but not before I kilt my daddy. He was a bad drunk. One night he took to whooping up on my mother and me. Damn! He was even mean when he wasn't drunk. I got even though. Maybe that's why I'm so mean, too," Jim chuckled.

"Naw, you were just born mean," replied Big Bob laughing.

After twenty minutes or so, the four guys that were standing at the bar decided to sit down at two tables next to Big Bob and Jim. They brought with them the two bottles of whiskey that they'd bought and started to get serious about doing some drinking.

"Hey, why don't we play some poker while we're waiting? I've got some cards right here in my pocket," suggested Dave.

"Can't you think of anything else besides playing poker?" Alfredo snapped.

"No, not really. I still want to try and get my money back from last night's game. You must've been cheating to have won that many hands."

"I don't have to cheat to beat a lousy poker player like you, Dave. Besides I don't think we'll be around this rinky-dink town long enough to do anything, let alone play poker."

"Hey, Big Bob, do we have enough time to play some poker before we get back on the trail?" asked Dave.

Big Bob looked over at the other table and replied, "Only if it's a fast game. We'll be in town for another hour tops. It shouldn't take much longer to fix my gun, but I need to pick up some supplies from the dry goods store before we go. You all stay here until I get back. I don't want you guys stinkin' drunk by the time we leave, so take it easy on the hooch. As soon as I finish this drink, I'll go see if my pistol is ready."

"You'd think Dave was made of money as much as he plays poker all the time. I guess he must break even a lot or he wouldn't keep trying to get guys to play," declared Jim.

"Yeah, maybe I can use him as a bank and just ask for withdrawals. Haw! Haw!" laughed Big Bob.

"You bet. The Lord giveth and Big Bob taketh away," Jim replied, laughing and slapping his knee.

"Yeah, well I guess I should stop lollygagging and go see if the gunsmith is done. Wait here for me here until I get back," ordered Big Bob, standing up and heading toward the front door.

Sheriff Anderson stopped working on his paperwork. He thought that he should probably take a stroll around town to make sure those riders he saw earlier were minding their own business. Richard pushed back his chair and got up from behind his oak desk but stopped before he started toward the front door.

Perhaps it might be a good idea to bring the double-barreled shotgun that normally stayed locked in the rifle rack by the door to the cells. There was hardly any trouble around these parts to warrant a larger jail or anything more than his pistol, but it might be wise to have a little extra firepower when confronting a large group of men. It might deter these guys from action if they were confronted by a lawman carrying a shotgun.

The sheriff stepped up to the gun rack and took his keys out of his pocket. He unlocked the big padlock holding the chain that went through three Winchester rifles and the side-by-side shotgun. Once he pulled out the shotgun, he replaced the chain and snapped the padlock shut.

Richard opened the double-barreled shotgun by pushing the swivel lever on top. This lever breaks the half holding the stock and hammer strikers away from the barrel section holding the shells. After he checked to be sure it was loaded, the sheriff decided to bring along some extra shells, just in case.

He unlocked the two-drawer file cabinet to look for the extra shells he kept for his pistols, rifles and the shotgun. He found the 12-gauge shells in the top drawer next to the rifle cartridge boxes, alongside two spare pistols he kept in the remote chance he would ever need them for a posse.

Richard stored his paper files in the lower drawer, so ammunition or weapons didn't get mixed up with paperwork. The sheriff was proud of this system. *'When things get desperate, there's no time to be searching around to locate shells or guns you need in a hurry.'* After removing a half dozen additional shotgun shells, Richard carefully relocked the file cabinet.

Sheriff Anderson pulled his Colt out of the holster to check whether he had five or six cartridges in the cylinder. Usually, he loaded only five, making sure that the one open chamber was placed directly behind the firing pin. That way, the gun wouldn't fire accidentally if it fell. As he opened the cartridge mechanism, Richard spun the cylinder and inserted a cartridge into the empty chamber just in case he might need it.

The sheriff also examined his gun belt to see if there were any empty cartridge loops that could hold additional bullets. Most gun belts have a row of twenty slots running around the back. Richard noticed seven empty loops, so he filled them from a box of cartridges he kept handy in his right top desk drawer. 'You never know what might happen and need extra bullets' he thought to himself.

Now that he felt as well prepared as possible, Sheriff Anderson left his office, locking the door behind him. He paused on the wooden planks in front of the jail to check in all directions for any unusual activity. As he looked to his right, Richard saw six horses tethered outside the saloon. 'That makes sense. They probably needed to wet their whistles after a long ride on the trail.'

As he crossed to the left side of the street headed toward the gun shop, the sheriff noticed a large man leaving the saloon. He stopped walking and stepped into the shadows beside the blacksmith shop to remain unseen as he observed the stranger's progress. As the tall man crossed the street and entered Tom's, Richard noticed that the fellow didn't have a leg iron in his holster, so he surmised that Tom was likely working on this guy's gun.

The sheriff decided that he would go down to Tom's and have a talk with this stranger to see how long he and his friends would be in town. Richard quickened his pace, so he would get to the gunsmith before the stranger came out.

As the sheriff entered, the cow bell sounded his presence. He heard the big fellow ask loudly, "When will you have my gun ready?" and Tom's reply that he would be finished in a few minutes and be right out.

Big Bob turned around quickly to see who had come into the shop after him. He spied a tall fellow wearing a badge and holding a shotgun in his left hand with the barrels pointed toward the floor. Immediately, Big Bob's right hand flew directly to his empty holster. Only after he remembered that he wasn't armed did he give the sheriff a slight grin. Big Bob had no love for lawmen, but he didn't want to make a scene without his favorite weapon at his disposal.

The sheriff noted the guy's edginess and the natural movement of his hand to the empty holster. Richard also noticed that the man wore his holster slung low on his right hip like most gunslingers and decided this might be one fellow to keep a close eye on. The sheriff looked directly into the fellow's eyes and said, "Howdy."

"Howdy yourself, Marshal."

"It's Sheriff, by the way. I saw you fellas come into town a while ago. You plan to be here long?"

"Nope. We just stopped to get a drink and some supplies, and get my gun fixed. Any harm in that, Sheriff?"

"No, no problem. I just want to know how long people plan on sticking around town is all. We get a lot of single people passing through these days, so a large group of men attracts attention."

"We won't give you no trouble, Sheriff. We're right peaceable kind of fellas."

"Okay, let's keep it that way." Raising his voice to be heard in back, the sheriff addressed the gunsmith, "Hey, Tom, is everything all right in here?"

"No problem here, Rich." Tom and Sheriff Anderson were best friends.

"Okay, Tom. I'll be back in a little while to talk to you, but I need to make my rounds first." The sheriff looked over at the stranger and declared, "I hope you enjoy your 'brief' stay in town, mister."

"We've enjoyed it so far, Sheriff. We hope to continue enjoying it for a little while longer," Big Bob replied with a little grin.

The sheriff furrowed his brows at the comment, then turned and strolled with deliberate ease out of the shop. He made a right as he stepped out of the doorway and continued down the street toward the livery stable. Richard wanted to talk to Jeb about getting a couple of horses to use when he and Cody went fishing later that afternoon.

But the sheriff's mind was more on the conversation he had just finished with the big stranger. He knew he didn't trust the man and certainly didn't like him. The guy rubbed him the wrong way. Richard had a gut feeling that something was just not right and made a mental note to keep a close eye on the stranger and his riding partners.

Big Bob turned impatiently back to the display case and demanded loudly, "Aren't you done yet?"

"I'm just putting the final touches on your gun." '*This fellow really does not like to be kept waiting and it makes me uneasy.*' A few minutes later, Tom finished the repairs and returned to the front counter. He handed the customer his pistol and told him to try the trigger action.

Big Bob cocked the hammer and pulled the trigger. It only took a light touch to make the hammer snap back into firing position. He test-fired the revolver several times and was pleased with the result. "This is fine," Big Bob finally announced with a satisfied grin. He immediately loaded the cylinder with cartridges from his gun belt, then spun it to make sure nothing hampered the mechanism. The chambers clicked by smoothly, and everything sounded right to gunslinger's practiced ear.

"That will be one dollar for the repair work, mister."

"That seems reasonable," declared Big Bob as he shoved his gun back into its holster. He took money from his pocket to pay the gunsmith, then turned with surprising quickness for a man of his size and marched out of the shop toward the dry goods store across the street.

Tom watched for a moment as the big man strode away and then went outside to look for the sheriff. He spotted Richard three doors down walking away from him. Tom yelled, "Hey, Rich!" and waited to see if the sheriff heard him. He must have yelled loudly enough, because Richard stopped walking, turned around and looked in his direction. Tom motioned for the sheriff to return. He wanted to have a talk with him about the customer he had just helped. Tom waited in the doorway as Sheriff Anderson made his way back up the street. Once Richard was close enough, Tom said quietly, "Let's talk inside."

"Okay by me," replied the sheriff as he followed Tom into the store.

After the gunsmith had taken only a few steps, he stopped and looked seriously at his friend. "Rich, I have a bad feeling about the guy that was just here."

"I know what you mean, Tom. I had the same feeling myself when I talked to him."

"What do you plan to do? It would be better for this town if that gunslinger and his pals didn't stick around very long."

"Yeah, I agree. I'll be keeping a close watch on that bunch. I have a bad feeling that something is going to happen soon. I'll see you later, Tom. I have to complete my rounds."

"Okay Rich. See you later," Tom hollered as the sheriff left the store.

While the sheriff and Tom were talking, Big Bob had enough time to buy some provisions at the dry goods store and return to the saloon. He returned to his seat next to Jim and poured himself another glass of whiskey.

"Did you get the .45 fixed the way you wanted?" asked his friend.

"Yup. It seems to be working good, Jim. Let's hope it stays that way."

"Yeah. It would be bad if it jammed at the wrong time."

About five minutes later as he was almost back to the jail, the sheriff heard increasingly loud voices coming from the saloon. He hurriedly crossed the street and stepped up onto the walkway in front. Richard could just see over the top of the swinging doors into the interior.

He noticed one of the strangers yelling at Clem to get away from their table. Evidently, the guy didn't appreciate a drunk trying to mooch drinks from them. The stranger stood up and pushed Clem roughly away from the table.

"You old barfly, git away from me!" shouted Dave. Clem was still unsteadily on his feet and again took a few steps toward their table. Dave moved quickly and shoved Clem even harder, sending him flying into the next table and onto the floor.

Pushing the right half of the swinging doors out of his way, Richard stepped into the saloon and declared, "Hey, that's enough of that. I'm the sheriff here and there's no need for violence." Ignoring the warning, Dave stomped angrily toward Clem and started viciously kicking him.

Sheriff Anderson quickly moved to Clem's side, spun Dave around and punched him in the jaw. This sent Dave flying onto his friends' table, knocking over all their drinks and flinging whiskey everywhere. Richard could tell that most of these men had swallowed enough whiskey to be drunk.

Dave scrambled to his feet, shouting, "Hey lawman, nobody hits me and gets away with it, most of all the law."

Richard hated to put down the shotgun but needed both hands to pull Clem from the floor. After putting the weapon on the table behind him, he leaned down and hauled Clem to his feet. The sheriff ordered him to go into the storage room at the back of the saloon, and Clem shuffled off.

In the livery stable, Jeb and Cody heard the growing commotion from the saloon. Cody had seen his father enter the place only moments earlier and ran full tilt toward the sound.

Jeb called out, "Cody wait. Come back here. We don't know what's going on in there!"

But Cody was too concerned to wait, and shouted, "I'll be back in a few minutes, Jeb. I want to see what's going on," as he raced toward his father. The boy literally leaped the last five feet onto the wooden walkway in front of the saloon. He was simultaneously excited and frightened as he peered over the swinging doors, trying to see what was happening.

"You bastard, I'll take care of you once and for all," snarled Dave. As the sheriff was turning from Clem to focus back on Dave, out of the corner of his eye he caught sight of the gunslinger drawing his revolver. Reaching for his own pistol, Richard whirled toward the impending danger.

As he spun, the sheriff snatched a brief glimpse at the others to see if they were also going for their guns. Thankfully, none of them had yet drawn. Depending on what happened with Dave, however, that might change quickly. He did not relish the idea of going up against six men, but it was far too late to worry about that now.

"Just for that Sheriff, I'm going to fill you full of holes," bellowed Dave, his rage growing by the second.

Cody could only stand outside the swinging doors, frozen with fear and watching in horror as everything unfolded before his eyes in sickening slow motion.

Dave's gun was just clearing his holster when the sheriff yelled, "Hold it! There is no need for this." The gunman noticed that the Colt .45 in the sheriff's right hand was already pointed squarely at him but continued his draw, getting off one quick shot. Reddish flames and gray smoke billowed from the end of his revolver as the bullet whizzed by the sheriff's left shoulder, tearing a hole in his shirt and putting a shallow two-inch furrow angling upward along his skin. Cody stared in disbelief as the bullet made a wrinkled pucker in his father's sleeve.

The sheriff had no choice but to put a bullet directly into the middle of Dave's chest, as orange flames belched from his .45. The retorts from the gunfire echoed loudly inside the saloon. Unable to move, Cody watched the bullet rip through Dave's white shirt, spewing ruby red blood into the air and soaking through the fabric.

The force of the impact threw the gunslinger back several feet. His arms flung outward, then dangled limply toward the ground. Unfortunately for him, Dave was already dead before he slumped to the floor and dropped his gun. Even after death, his trigger finger continued twitching. Five chairs flew backward as the other gang members jumped to their feet, drawing their weapons as they rose.

"Dad watch out!" Cody screamed helplessly.

From the positioning of the three tables, the remaining gunmen made a lethal half-circle in front of the sheriff. '*Dammit!*' Aware this was probably the end of his life, the sheriff attempted to take as many of the gunslingers with him as he could, fanning his gun at the gang.

As his dad blasted away, Cody saw him hit Jorge high in the left shoulder. Jorge's shirt wrinkled and dust rose into the air as the bullet entered his body. A fountain of crimson blood immediately spurted from the impact hole. Grunting in pain, Jorge was jerked backward to the right. His pistol discharged before it fell to the floor, hitting the sheriff in the upper left arm above the elbow.

This slowed the sheriff's movement and threw off his aim, but he managed to hit Alfredo's right ear close to the lobe. Following the bullets trajectory, a scarlet spray of blood flew backward from the wound as the torn skin wobbled loosely back and forth. Alfredo yelled, "Damn!" as his left hand went up to cover his injured ear.

Big Bob and Jim fired together, hitting Richard twice in the left side of his chest and puncturing his lung near the heart. The sheriff continued shooting even as he fell to the floor, hitting the whiskey bottle on their table and spraying both Big Bob and Jim with glass and whiskey.

Every second seemed like an hour to the terrified teenager as the bullets struck his dad. Cody watched his father's shirtfront pucker as the bullets hit him, blood spraying out of the holes and soaking the right side of his shirt.

Screaming, "Dad! Dad!" Cody tried to rush into the fray to somehow help his father, but Jeb had finally reached his side and held the boy in a viselike grip to prevent him from entering the saloon.

The anguished teen continued to struggle as Jeb yelled, "No, Cody. You'll only get killed if you go in there now!"

The sheriff had fallen to the floor on his left side. Once the firing stopped and the thunderous roar of gunshots faded, an eerie silence fell over the saloon, broken only by the mortally-wounded lawman's hoarse whisper, "Cody." The sheriff lay groaning on the floor, eventually turning onto his back. None of the gunmen bothered to fire at him again since they knew Sheriff Anderson would soon be dead.

As Cody squirmed in Jeb's embrace sobbing, "Dad, what have you done to my dad?" the bartender rose slowly from behind bar and looked warily back and forth, hoping the shooting was finally over.

Jorge swore loudly about his shoulder and sat back down at his table wondering if there was a doctor in town. Alfredo holstered his gun and continued to hold his bleeding ear, wondering the same thing.

By now, the sheriff was unconscious and very close to death. His blood had pooled on the floor around him and turned his entire shirtfront a garish red. Cody finally broke free from Jeb's grasp and threw open the saloon door, racing headlong to his father's side. Everyone's attention turned in Cody's direction as he knelt sobbing by his father, cradling his dad's broken body in his arms as the sheriff died.

Big Bob holstered his gun and declared, "We need to get out of here as fast as we can. We don't know what the townspeople or any deputies might do now that their sheriff is dead. We can stitch up our wounds after we put some distance between us and this town." Jim examined Jorge's wounded shoulder and announced that he could ride.

Cody looked up briefly and scanned the gang's faces intently. "You murdered my father. I will remember each and every last one of you, and I am going to kill you all."

"Sure kid, and we'll be waiting for you. Haw! Haw!" chuckled Jim, grinning wickedly.

"I don't care if it takes the rest of my life, but I'll get you." Still crying, Cody turned back to his father. Jeb cautiously entered the saloon, skirting the tables to reach Cody while keeping a watchful eye on the gunmen.

"All right fellas. Let's get going!" shouted Jim as he pushed Alfredo toward the door. Since his friend was light-headed from loss of blood, Rick held a still-swearing Jorge around the waist to steady him.

The gunslingers hightailed it from the saloon and mounted their horses, Rick helping Jorge into the saddle. They galloped fast, heading east toward Colorado and were soon out of sight.

Cody sat weeping, staring down at his dead father for several minutes. Jeb tried unsuccessfully to coax him away from the sheriff's bloody, bullet-ridden body.

"Come along, Cody. There's nothing we can do for your father now. We'll get Jose to come and get his body and build a coffin," continued Jeb gently. Jose Sanchez, a local carpenter, handled the responsibilities of town undertaker. Jeb instructed the bartender to have Clem fetch Jose and some others to take care of the bodies.

"Leave me alone, Jeb." Cody refused to leave his father's side until Jose and the others arrived.

The Wilsons and their patrons heard the horrific gun battle and huddled together in terror. After Richard left his shop, Tom had gone to the restaurant to grab some lunch. As soon as the gunmen were out of sight, he and the Wilsons rushed over to the saloon to see what had happened. Tom was sorry to find his friend lying dead on the floor with Cody bawling at his side.

Tom entered the saloon, put a comforting hand on Cody's shoulder, and declared, "Cody, I'm so sorry for what happened." Months earlier, Richard had asked Tom to take care of his son if he were ever killed because Cody didn't have any other living family. Tom had promised that he'd keep a roof over Cody's head and provide food for his belly until his eighteenth birthday. Sadly, neither man knew that fate would so quickly intervene exactly as the sheriff had feared.

It took several minutes for Clem to return with Jose and three helpers. Jose approached Cody, leaned down and said softly, "I'm sorry Cody that this happened. Me and these hombres are here to take your father and prepare him for burial." The group came forward and gathered around the fallen sheriff. After each man took a limb, they slowly lifted the body and moved solemnly out the swinging saloon doors.

Jeb and Tom helped Cody off the floor and followed behind the group carrying his father.

Once outside, Cody brokenheartedly watched the sad procession move down the street toward Jose's place.

Tom spoke gently, "Cody, let's go back to your house. You can rest, and I can fix you something to eat."

"Yeah, that's a good idea," agreed Jeb. "Don't worry about anything at the livery stable for a while. I can handle it."

Cody didn't say anything but slowly nodded his head, numb from the shock of his father's horrific death. He was still sniffling with tears streaming unheeded down his face.

Once they arrived at the house, Tom softly pushed Cody through the door and led him to his bedroom. Cody sat woodenly on the bed and Tom suggested, "Why don't you rest a while?"

"How can I rest when my life as I know it is over?"

"I know you're hurting fierce right now, but things will get better in time. Your dad and I had a conversation a while back, and I promised him that I'd look after you."

Looking sternly up at Tom, Cody announced, "I don't need anyone looking out for me. I can take care of myself."

The gunsmith gave Cody a small, sympathetic smile and replied, "You may think that now, but you are still too young to go out on your own. Just lay down and try and rest. I'll check on you a little later to see how you're doing." Tom turned away and quietly left the room, closing the door behind him. He hoped Cody would get some rest, but he doubted it.

Cody raised his legs onto the bed, turned his face to the wall and sobbed bitterly. He missed his father terribly and now he was all alone in the world. The crying, grief and shock of seeing his father killed soon made him tired and, mercifully, Cody dozed off for about an hour.

But it was not a restful sleep. Images of the gun battle and his father's death flooded through his mind. In Cody's dreams, he tried again and again to save his dad, but nothing changed the outcome.

About forty-five minutes later, Tom heard a knock at the front door. He rose quickly from the table, hoping the noise wouldn't disturb Cody in the other room. When Tom opened the door, he faced a somber Emma and John Wilson.

"Why don't you come in for a few minutes, but please try and keep your voices down. I just got Cody to rest and I hope he is sleeping off the shock of today's sad events."

"Thanks Tom. We'll be quiet. We brought some food," declared Emma.

"We feel awful about Cody. Is there anything that we can do to help?" added John.

"Thanks, but there isn't anything anyone can do right now. We'd surely appreciate some of your fine vittles in the future though, Emma."

"You just let me know Tom. I'll make sure you and the boy don't go hungry."

Tom thanked the Wilsons again and saw them to the door. He returned to his seat at the table and patiently waited for Cody to come out of his room.

Cody woke with a jolt from the recurring nightmare of his father's murder. He was soaked with sweat and sat up shakily on the side of the bed. Breathing deeply, Cody put his face in his hands and bent over, supporting his elbows on his knees.

It took a few minutes to calm himself. He still missed his dad like crazy, but now he was angry, too. Cody was so filled with rage that he decided to ride after and confront the men who murdered his father before they got too far ahead.

Cody got to his feet to set his plan into action. He'd need to pack some clothes and get some food from the kitchen. But first, he ought to get the spare pistol and ammunition from his father's bedroom. Cody strode purposefully to the bedroom door, threw it open and stepped into the main room, but paused when he noticed Tom at the kitchen table.

Tom looked up when Cody entered the room and asked, "How are you feeling? Did you get any sleep?"

"Yeah, I got some, but it didn't do much good because I dreamed about my father's murder. Now I've decided to set off after those men and kill every last one of them."

"Are you nuts, boy? They'll eat you for breakfast and not even think twice about killing you! Your father told me you've barely even learned how to shoot a gun. You don't have any chance at all to draw and fire fast enough to kill a gang of gunslingers."

Intent on revenge, Cody continued toward Richard's room. "I don't care. I have to do something, and this seems right to me."

Tom rose and followed the boy into his father's room. "Cody, your plan isn't gonna work. You won't even the score by getting yourself killed."

Ignoring Tom's advice, Cody hurried to his father's desk and opened the bottom drawer where he kept his backup gun and spare bullets. As he pulled out the pistol, Tom snatched it from his hands.

Cody shouted, "Give that back to me!" and lunged for the weapon, but Tom kept it out of reach.

"If I can take this gun from your hand so easily, then you have no business using it. If you'll calm down a minute and let me talk to you, maybe we can work something out."

"I don't want to work something out! I want to kill them all now."

"I'll make you a deal. If you work with me, I'll train you correctly and you'll have a much better chance of killing those men and getting out alive."

"But I'm angry now and I want satisfaction."

Tom shook his head and declared, "I know you're angry, but we can use that to our advantage. Hate will make you work harder and it may take you less time to complete your training. Come into the kitchen and sit down with me so I can explain what you'll need to learn."

"I'll listen, but what if I don't agree with your plan? How long do you expect me to wait?"

They both entered the kitchen and stood by the table. "To start with, sit down and I'll get you some water." After Cody took a seat, Tom brought him a glass of water. Cody drank it while he waited for Tom to speak.

"All right. First and perhaps most important, you must accept the idea that you don't yet know everything about firearms, especially about drawing down on and killing a man. After that, you must master three skills to be a successful marksman. One: Shoot accurately with both hands in case you get wounded in one arm or the other. Two: Handle a rifle just as well as a pistol for long-range shots. Three: Throw a knife proficiently with both hands as a backup if you're caught without your guns or run out of bullets."

"Cody, I'm willing to train you and teach you those skills. Now, have you understood everything

I've said, or are you going out unprepared and get yourself killed? It's your choice, but I know which option I'd pick."

Cody sat silently for a minute weighing Tom's offer against his pressing need to go after the killers. "You know, Tom, you've made some valid points and I'm not ready to die, so I'm willing to agree with your plan for my training. How soon can we start?"

With a sigh of relief, Tom replied, "We can start tomorrow. I'll have to send away for two pistols and a double-rig holster for you. You can repay me a little at a time from your job at the livery stable. I have a used pistol and holster that you can practice with until the new items come into my shop. We'll start your training tomorrow after you've finished working at the stable."

Cody leaned back in the chair and asked softly, "Where am I going to live? Can I stay here?"

"You're gonna live with me. The town will probably want this house for the next sheriff. We can move whatever belongings you'd like to keep over to my place in a day or two after your dad's funeral. I can store your things until you need them. If you'd like, we can sell your dad's clothes and other household items you don't want."

"Thanks Tom, but I don't think I want much from our house except my clothes and my father's watch. We can sell everything else so that I can help pay you back for your purchases and the funeral costs."

"Okay, we'll do it your way then. I'll get the word out to everyone in town about a possible sale. Right now, we'll stay in your house until the funeral."

The next morning after breakfast, Tom and Cody went through the house picking which items would go and which Cody wanted to keep. Once they were finished, Tom declared, "You don't have to go into work for a while, but I need to get to my shop. Why don't you come with me?"

"We can find a weapon and holster for you to use during practice. You won't need bullets yet. First, you must get comfortable gripping a pistol in the holster and pulling it out while working the mechanisms. Over time, I'll also teach you how to clean, oil and repair guns."

"That's fine. The sooner we get started, the sooner I can go after my dad's killers."

"Don't be in such a hurry or whatever I teach you will be for naught."

Cody and Tom left the house together and headed toward the gunsmith's shop. They were only steps from the entrance when Cody spotted his best friend, George Jackson, helping his father load some seed bags and chicken wire from Smith's Dry Goods into their wagon. George told his dad that he wanted to speak with Cody and would be back shortly. Cody advised Tom that he'd join him in the shop in a few minutes. The classmates met in the middle of Main Street.

"Cody, I'm real sorry about what happened to your dad. How are you doing?"

"I'm still pretty upset and angry. I guess it's going to take some time. Dad's funeral will be tomorrow or the next day."

"Is there anything I can do for you?"

"No, but thanks for asking. You might mention the funeral to our classmates and the rest of the school."

"I'll let everyone know. I've got to help my dad now, so I'll talk to you later," George declared, waving as he ran back to his father's wagon.

"See yah," replied Cody as he crossed the street and entered Tom's shop. Like most structures in Shiprock, it was built of adobe.

Unlike the other stores, however, it was heavily fortified to protect against would-be burglars. The store's single window was covered with narrowly spaced metal bars to prevent anyone from crawling through it.

The only entrance, the dark brown front door, was constructed of sturdy two-inch thick oak. It had both a key lock and a metal hinged lock two-thirds of the way up, making it very difficult to steal the expensive weapons inside.

Cody had often visited the store over the years and enjoyed looking at the weapons on display almost as much as he liked examining the selection of candy lined up along one counter in the dry goods store. Today, Cody peered into the glass display cases and imagined using the knives and guns to kill the men who murdered his father.

Tom quietly studied Cody from his work area in the back. "Hey Cody, why don't you come back here? We can search for a gun and holster for you."

"Okay. I was just looking at all the beautiful guns in the displays." Eager to get even a practice pistol into his hands, Cody trotted into Tom's workroom.

The back room had a work bench running the entire length of the right wall, filled with Tom's tools and spare gun parts. Boxes of screws, pins, springs, gun barrels, grips and other items from various gun makers packed two additional shelves below the bench.

On the left wall were three cabinets. The tallest contained rifles beneath two upper shelves loaded with extra cartridges. The next six-shelf cabinet held pistols on the bottom four shelves with additional boxes of bullets on the top two. These could both be padlocked shut. The final cabinet had a large array of holsters and knives.

"Cody, open the last cabinet and check the lower shelves for a very worn holster. You might have to dig around to find it. I'll get you a used revolver from the pistol cabinet."

Cody bent over and began searching through the piles of black, deep brown and tan gun belts on the second shelf. He even found one medium gray holster but saw nothing resembling what Tom had described. After fruitlessly examining every belt on the shelf, Cody knelt to rummage through the bottom.

Cody finally found it tucked away in the back beneath two other holsters. Tom said it was pretty used and the belt certainly looked that way. The battered right-handed one-gun holster had lost most of its original dark brown color and looked even lighter than the newer tan belts. It had scratches all over the holster from excessive wear, and tears on both the top and bottom sides of the strap, most likely from hanging it on a hook. Cody held up the gun belt and asked, "Tom, is this the holster you were talking about?"

Tom took a quick glance and responded, "That's the one. Pretty isn't it?"

"I think you and I have different ideas about what's pretty," Cody chuckled.

As he returned to his search for the pistol he wanted for Cody, Tom added, "It'll suit our purposes for now." It took Tom several minutes to find the revolver, hidden behind some pistols on the lower shelf. If someone wanted a cheap gun, this would certainly be it.

The 1851 cap and ball Colt .38 revolver weighed a whopping 2.6 pounds, more than twice as heavy and two inches longer than the current 1873 single-action Colt pistol. The gun had lost the bluing on its barrel and cartridge cylinder over the years and was now a sickly dull gray, a far cry from the shiny deep blue of the newer model.

"Here she is! Isn't she great?" Tom joshed.

"My God! Does that thing even work?" Cody exclaimed. He took it reluctantly from Tom's hand.

"Yes, it works, but that's not the point. I won't have to worry if something bad happens to it or the gun gets lost. It's the heaviest and longest weapon that I have in stock, perfect for practicing. It's best to start learning with the heaviest gun. When your pistols arrive, they'll feel considerably lighter and you'll be able to pull them measurably faster."

"Why don't you buckle on the belt and holster the pistol right now? You can start getting the feel of wearing them, so you can get used to the weight. You'll want the belt to be rather snug against your body, so that it doesn't slide around."

Cody put the revolver in the holster and slung the gun belt around his waist. Most belts have six holes for the belt buckle to go through. Cody put the buckle through the fourth slot and found it to be fairly comfortable.

Tom approached to check the fit, tugging the belt back and forth across Cody's hips. "Well, it fits pretty good for what we need. You may want to lower the right side a bit, so you can more easily reach the handle. The grip should be the same height as your hand as it lays comfortably against your right side. This makes it much easier and quicker to draw the pistol from the holster than wasting valuable time having to reach further up to grab the grip."

"That makes a lot of sense Tom. Wearing a rig does feel a little strange. I didn't have the chance to use a gun belt when dad took me shooting. He just showed me how to load and fire the pistol."

"Don't worry about that now. You need to get the feel of wearing the belt most of the time, especially here in the shop and at our house. It's gonna take a while to get comfortable with this setup. You can begin practicing by grabbing the gun and pulling it from the holster. The idea is to make the draw become second nature and become faster each time you complete the repetition. This will take many months to perfect and possibly years to become very fast."

"I can see that this will take time, but I'm up for it." Cody felt complete now, all grown up like the other men who wore guns around town.

"Cody, I need to work on a couple of weapons that have come in for repair. Why don't you practice in the store for a while? If someone comes in, you can holler for me or try to help them yourself. I can use your assistance selling guns and knives, while you become familiar with different calibers and types of weapons."

"I'd also like you to clean the glass on the cabinets and keep everything straight in the displays. I think we should put price cards next to each item in the cases. That way, customers won't have to ask how much anything costs. I saw that advertising trick in a gun shop the last time I visited Tucson. I wanted to try it here, but I haven't had time to do it."

"That's a good idea Tom. I'd be glad to help." Like most boys his age, Cody was fascinated by guns. 'Now,' he thought, 'I'll be able to touch, hold and sell them for Tom.'

Tom returned to his work bench, positioned his angular frame on his tall stool and began disassembling a pistol to get to its firing pin. It was a common repair - if someone used their gun often, the pin would have to be replaced regularly.

Cody began practicing drawing the revolver. After a while, he realized the grip was too far from his hand and readjusted his belt downward to a more comfortable position. No one came into the shop all day, although Cody saw a fair number of locals moving around town, either going to Smith's Dry Goods or visiting the restaurant for food.

Cody kept practicing, holding his hand out slightly from the gun rig and slapping it as fast as he could to grab the grip. Sometimes, he'd bend his knees slightly and turn his body just a bit as he pulled the gun out of its holster. He pretended to point it at people who passed by the window, careful that they wouldn't see him. "Hey Tom, how soon before we can go out of town to teach me to shoot?"

"Probably sometime later next week, Cody. Until then, just keep practicing grabbing the gun. It's a very important skill. Soon we'll practice drawing faster than you're doing now. You'll also need to pull back the firing pin at the same time as you draw the revolver from the holster. It takes a lot of practice to make that action smooth and fast."

It was almost five o'clock when Tom finished for the day. He took a few more minutes to clean up his work bench and stow his tools where he could find them tomorrow. Tom had a little satchel with extra tools in case he was called to one of the local ranches to make repairs. Thankfully, that didn't happen often. He'd watched Cody practicing from the workshop and noticed the boy had been carefully studying all the different handguns in the cases.

Most of these were black powder pistols. Tom did not sell as many of these older models now, with the newer single action guns being produced. The older revolvers required a primer cap be attached to a circular nipple. Once struck by the firing pin, the cap would send a fiery spark into black powder packed into each cylinder and held in place above the bullet by a paper wad.

The recent invention of individual bullet casings to hold the primer and the explosive powder made shooting a revolver much less dangerous, but there was still a chance that the cylinder or barrel might rupture and injure the shooter if the casings were overloaded or the powder was improperly mixed.

"Cody, I'm done here today. Why don't we go eat at Wilson's before we head back to your house?" suggested Tom as he used a cloth from the workshop to remove the dirt, black powder and oil from his hands.

"That sounds good to me. I'm pretty hungry right about now. I didn't eat too much last night or this morning on account of being upset over my dad's death."

Tom stood by the workshop sink. "You can wash your hands back here before we eat. Leave your rig here. We'll stop back by the shop to pick it up after supper, so you can practice some more tonight."

"All right. That sounds good to me too." After Cody finished washing up, Tom locked the shop door and they headed down the street to get dinner at the restaurant.

"Let's get steak and potatoes. Boy am I hungry!" exclaimed Tom.

When Tom and Cody strolled through the restaurant door, the place was about a one-third full. Everyone turned around to see who had entered, and most folks rose from their seats to greet them. Although everyone was sympathetic, patting Cody's shoulder or shaking his hand as they expressed their regrets for the sheriff's untimely passing, the boy was confused and a little uncomfortable with all the attention.

Mrs. Wilson was serving a couple their dinner when she noticed what was happening and took it upon herself to let the other customers know that they shouldn't bother Cody too much right now. To keep an eye on the boy and let them both eat in peace, Emma led Tom and Cody to a table near the kitchen. She then handed them menus and put a pitcher of water and two glasses on the table. Wilson's offered the standard fare of most restaurants in the Southwest at this time:

Wilson's Restaurant

Boiled Mutton with Oyster Sauce	10¢
Roast Beef with Lima Beans or Peas	10¢
Beefsteak & Onions with Fried Potatoes	10¢
Stewed Mutton with Bread, Butter & Potatoes	5¢
Buckwheat Cakes with Honey	5¢
Chicken Pot Pie	20¢
Porterhouse Steak	25¢
Roast Turkey and Currant Jelly	25¢
Hot Oatmeal Mush	10¢

"Thanks for the menus, Emma. Cody and I will each have the porterhouse steak and potatoes. If you have any of your wonderful biscuits left, we'll take some of those too."

"Okay, gentlemen. I'll start on your food directly."

Tom and Cody waited only a short while before their meals arrived. In the meantime, more people entered the restaurant and stared at Cody. He continued to feel a little self-conscious about all the looks he was getting.

"Don't worry about being gawked at. Folks are just feeling sorry for you," explained Tom. Cody sighed, but didn't answer.

As Mrs. Wilson brought their steaming plates of food she asked, "Is there anything else that I can get you?"

"No thanks, but this food sure does look good," replied Cody.

"You're welcome to it Cody. Now you just relax and eat up. I've made a little snack for the two of you for later," Mrs. Wilson added, smiling kindly. They ate in silence for almost ten minutes.

Cody finished first, patted his belly and declared, "Thanks Tom. That was really good."

"You are certainly welcome. I wish we could eat here every day, but it's too expensive to do this all the time." It took Tom several more minutes to finish his meal. He waved Mrs. Wilson over to the table after she'd finished serving another customer.

"Gosh, Emma, that was really good! I might steal you away from John," teased Tom.

"Oh, go on with you, Tom. John would like that anyway. Then he could play poker in the saloon all the time," laughed Mrs. Wilson.

"How much do we owe you?" asked Tom.

"That's seventy cents total. Just wait a minute and I'll go get your goodies that I baked."

After paying Mrs. Wilson and grabbing the bag of sweets, they left the restaurant and headed back to the shop to pick up Cody's practice rig.

Once they reached Cody's house, Tom recommended that he strap on the rig and practice his draw for at least an hour or two before bed. A half hour later there was a knock at the door. Tom rose from the table where he had been reading a book and watching Cody practice. He opened it and found Jose standing there.

"Hey Jose, how are you?"

"Hi Tom, hey Cody."

"You're welcome to join us," invited Tom.

"Cody what are you doing?" asked Jose as he stepped into the house.

"I'm learning to draw a gun, so that I can kill the men who murdered my father."

"Aren't you a little young for that?"

"I have to start sometime. It might as well be now."

Jose shook his head doubtfully, not sure what to make of that. "Anyway, Tom, we're ready for Richard's burial tomorrow, if that suits you."

Tom looked silently at Cody for a moment, "How do you feel about that Cody?"

"Tomorrow is fine by me. Will it work for you, Tom?"

"Sure Cody. Say Jose, what time were you thinking of holding the burial?"

"We could do it one of two ways, either at 9:00 in the morning so it won't be too hot, or else around 6:30 in the evening when the sunset is pretty and its cooled off some."

"Cody, what do you think your dad would prefer?"

"I think he'd like evening best. Dad always enjoyed watching the sunset, and that will give us time to spread the word around town to people who might want to come."

Tom nodded in agreement. "I think you made a good choice."

"All right, fellas. Evening it is then. I'll have everything ready and start getting the word out to everyone. Well, Cody, you just carry on with what you were doing, and I'll see you tomorrow. I sure am sorry about your dad," declared Jose as he turned toward the door.

"Thanks, Jose. Good night," replied Cody.

"Good night," Jose responded as he left the house.

The next day was pretty much a repeat of the day before. A few people came to the shop to look at some of the guns and talk to Tom. Others dropped by to extend their condolences to Cody.

Cody continued his practice, slapping his hand to the gun butt and drawing it from the holster. The repetition was making it easier and his draw was becoming a little faster each day, but Cody knew he still had a long way to go before his training would be complete and he could fire a weapon with deadly accuracy.

Tom's voice interrupted his thoughts. "Cody, it's almost time for the funeral. Do you have a suit to wear?"

"No, I haven't had a suit since I was about eight years old. I do have a nice pair of gray pants and a clean white shirt though."

"I guess that'll do. I can let you borrow a tie for the funeral to spruce things up a bit. Why don't you stop practicing and go home and change? I'll go to my place and meet you at your house after I get into my suit."

As he unbuckled the gun belt and handed it to Tom, Cody replied, "Okay, that sounds good. Dad has a black cloth western tie that I'd like to wear to the funeral. I'll wait for you at the house." Cody left the shop and headed home.

Twenty minutes later, Tom arrived at Cody's house wearing a light brown suit and a dark brown cloth tie. Cody thought Tom cut a fine figure.

After struggling unsuccessfully with his father's tie, Cody asked, "Tom, can you please help me with this? Dad always tied one for me if I needed it."

"Sure. Come stand in front of me and I'll fix it for you." Tom was finished in less than a minute. Cody took a deep breath and prepared himself for the ordeal to come. He thought sadly, 'once dad is buried next to mom, I'll be the last survivor of the Anderson family.' The idea made Cody feel sad and small. He realized just how much he owed to Tom Haines.

Tom and Cody left the house together and walked west toward the cemetery on the outskirts of town. As they neared the jail, they noticed that most of the locals had already gathered on Main Street. All the businesses in Shiprock were closed due to the funeral of one of the town's most beloved citizens. They acknowledged everyone as they led the group on the three-minute walk out to the cemetery.

Harold Webster, the town pastor, was waiting at the burial site where Cody's father would be lowered into the sandy soil. Jose's men had already dug a six-foot deep cavity for the wooden casket, three feet wide by six and a half feet long. Before the service, the coffin rested on two wooden poles over the hole. Afterwards, Jose's men would use long ropes to lower the casket into the ground.

The mourners stood in a circle around the coffin. Once everyone stopped moving, Pastor Webster began the eulogy. As tears welled in Cody's eyes, he brought up his left arm to wipe his face on his sleeve. After the pastor led the final hymn and everyone said, "Amen," he came over to Cody and squeezed the boy's shoulder.

"I am sorry for the loss of your father. He was a good man. Everyone loved and respected him, and we will all miss him."

Tom and Cody remained silently by the grave as most of the townspeople began to leave the cemetery. John and Emma Wilson quietly approached and advised that they had set up light refreshments for everyone at their restaurant. Tom thanked them and assured the Wilsons that he and Cody would be along shortly.

Once they were by themselves, Cody half-whispered, "Tom, I'd like to be alone for a few minutes."

"Take as much time as you need. I'll be waiting at the entrance to the cemetery."

Cody walked closer and knelt by his father's wooden casket, placing his hand on the lid. As his tears continued to fall, he began to speak, "Dad, I miss you so much. I don't know right now what's to become of me and my life, but I promise you this - I am going to avenge your death. By God's grace, I am going to kill those bastards, every last one of them." Cody then reached into his right pocket, pulled out his father's spare sheriff's badge and placed it sideways on the coffin lid.

"After I've killed them, I will put one of these badges on each of the men that murdered you. I love you and mom very much, and I'll try to visit you both as often as I can." With that, Cody rose and moved somberly away from his parents' graves.

Cody met Tom at the cemetery entrance and the two began walking back into town toward Wilson's restaurant.

"How are you holding up, Cody?"

"I'll be fine, but it may take some time."

The Wilsons served lemonade and butter cookies to the people of the town after the service. Tom and Cody sat at a centrally located table in the restaurant, so that people could stop by to pay their condolences and chat.

Most folks milled around in small groups talking about what happened and other issues of interest in their lives. Although he was still uncomfortable with all the attention, Cody was very pleased that most of the town had turned out to pay their respects to his father.

Cody leaned toward Tom and whispered, "I guess dad was more popular around here than I thought."

"He sure was. Your father was always kind to everyone around town. He helped people whenever he could and protected their stores, belongings and families. I never once heard anything bad said about him. You should be very proud of your dad."

"I am."

The gathering lasted about an hour before people began to leave. Once most of the locals had gone, Tom and Cody rose from their seats and approached Mrs. Wilson. Cody began by thanking her very much for everything they had done for his dad and for him. He then handed her a few dollars from his pants pocket to help pay for the expenses of the food and drink.

"No Cody, I can't accept your money," refused Emma Wilson, shaking her head.

"I know that mom and dad wouldn't want you to pay for all of this, so I must insist. It's all I can afford right now, but you can get back to me with how much I still owe."

"Don't be silly, Cody. We thank you. This is very generous and will cover the cost completely." Cody wasn't sure if Mrs. Wilson was telling the truth but decided to let it go at that. Tom said his goodbyes and Cody thanked the Wilsons again as they left and headed back to Cody's house.

"Cody, we'll move your stuff over to my place tomorrow. We can hold the sale of the other furniture and things here this weekend. I've already told everyone at the restaurant and they promised to spread the word."

"That sounds good, Tom. We can move my stuff in the morning before we go to the shop."

At the house, Cody first sorted through his belongings and packed the clothes he liked into a carpet bag that his father had used when he travelled, leaving behind others he'd outgrown or never wore. Then, he and Tom went through his father's things, starting with the six-foot high armoire. From there, Cody kept only a pair of dark gray slacks and a fancy western shirt his father wore when he took his mom out on special occasions. The shirt had mother-of-pearl buttons and was a beautiful smoky gray with vertical silver threads set every six inches across it.

Finally, Cody went through the chest of drawers. He kept a pair of long underwear and some socks. Everything else was put aside for the sale, including some of his mother's clothes that his father had kept. Cody also found two additional boxes of .45 caliber bullets. Tom said that he'd exchange them for others that would fit Cody's practice pistol.

The next day, Cody and Tom laid out the sale clothes on the table. Since the armoire and dresser were empty, they could be sold too. The sale was set for nine o'clock Saturday morning. Tom went to the shop while Cody worked a half-day at the stable moving hay bales and grain bags, mucking stalls and filling the feed bins for each horse.

Cody had asked Jeb some time ago about the possibility of helping with the blacksmithing duties. Today, Jeb announced that he could use extra help and it was time to teach Cody how to make horseshoes. They walked together into the blacksmith shop, and Jeb instructed Cody to watch closely as he made a horseshoe.

Jeb had already preheated the forge, using a large bellows to help the coals heat more quickly. The blacksmith kept a small stack of thin iron bars off in the back corner. He selected one and shoved it about a foot and a half into the coals. It took a minute before the rod glowed bright red. Using long-handled tongs, Jeb pulled out the rod to check that the color was perfect.

As the rod was too long for a horseshoe, the blacksmith used his big scissors to cut off a foot-long section and cooled the rest in a half-barrel filled with water. The rod sizzled, and steam rose into the air as droplets of water popped to the ground. The remaining red-hot piece was now ready to shape.

Jeb placed the fiery iron on the pointed end of the anvil, then instructed Cody to fetch the hammer and gently hit the end of the rod while rotating it slowly on its thin side. Gradually, the rod began to curve. Jeb reheated it in the forge, so it would bend more easily while working with it. The blacksmith pulled the curved rod from the fire and returned it to the anvil. Cody began striking it again and soon had shaped the iron into a rough approximation of a horseshoe.

"I'll take it from here," declared Jeb. Cody handed him the hammer and the blacksmith expertly closed the angle of the horseshoe to the correct degree, then pushed it back into the coals to reheat again.

This time, Jeb placed the flat face of the shoe onto the square end of the anvil, making sure only a short portion hung barely off the side. He banged the hammer a few more times to put a quarter-inch bend on the end and repeated the process for the other end.

Jeb again reheated the shoe, then used a punch he kept in a convenient hole on the side of the anvil to drive holes through it. This allowed small nails to be driven into a horse's hoof to hold the shoe snugly in place. Jeb dropped the completed horseshoe into the water barrel to cool off. Cody enjoyed working with the blacksmith to create a horseshoe. Hopefully, he would soon be making more. But now it was time to quit work and head to the gun shop.

Cody hurried to the store. The cowbell sounded when he entered, and Tom peeked out of the workroom. When he saw that it was Cody, he declared, "I have to finish some repairs. Why don't you strap on your holster and start practicing your quick draw?"

"Okay. Tom, how long do you think it will be before my guns and holster come?"

"It may take up to two months before the stage brings them into town."

"Well, I guess that's not too long. I wish it were sooner, though. I can't wait."

Tom had ordered two new Colt single-action .44 caliber pistols and a new double-holstered gun belt for Cody shortly after his father's death.

"When are we going out to practice shooting?"

"After the sale tomorrow. Go ahead and practice for a few hours inside and we'll close a half-hour early today to go eat."

Cody located the practice rig on top of the tallest workroom cabinet. He wrapped the gun belt around his hips, closing it on the fourth hole. He then strapped the bottom leather ties around his leg and lowered the right side of the belt to the proper height.

Cody practiced for about four hours. His speed draw was improving but pulling the hammer back at the same time was still challenging. Cody figured it wouldn't be too much longer before he perfected it. At about 4:30, Tom announced it was time to stop and put things away.

While unbuckling his gun belt, Cody remarked, "Tom, I believe that I could draw faster if I didn't have such a long revolver."

"Yeah, that's true, but it's better to practice first and get faster with this longer, heavier gun. That way, by the time you start practicing with your new pistols, they'll feel much lighter. All right. If you're ready, let's get going. We can eat a sandwich for dinner. How does that sound?"

"A sandwich is okay with me as long as we get to eat some of Mrs. Wilson's cookies for dessert."

It was two days after the gunfight in the saloon, and the gunmen had put over thirty miles between them and Shiprock. The next place they stopped was Farmington, New Mexico, a larger town of about three hundred people.

Jorge hoped they had a local sawbones. His shoulder ached like mad and continued to bleed during their ride. Both Jim and Big Bob offered to fish out the bullet, but Jorge didn't trust either one of them enough to do the procedure.

He kept his arm in a makeshift sling, so it wouldn't move so much during the journey. All his companions were sick of his complaining, so he had taken to riding further back behind the rest of them. By this time, Jorge had spiked a fever from the bullet in his shoulder. It's a good thing for him that the gang made town when they did.

The group pulled up in front of one of the local saloons at the edge of town. They all dismounted except Jorge, who wanted to stay in the saddle until he found the doctor's office. Big Bob ordered Alfredo to take Jorge to the doctor. They'd wait for him in the saloon until he returned. Alfredo entered the saloon to find out if there was a doctor in Farmington. All the others followed closely behind him, thirsty for a drink after the long ride.

"Hey barkeep, I'm looking fer a sawbones. Is there one close by?"

"You're in luck, mister. Doc Martin's office is only about two hundred yards straight down Main Street. Look for a white house on the right with a sign hanging outside with his name on it."

"All right," replied Alfredo, heading back outside. "Hey, Jim, I found a doctor. I'll drop Jorge off and be right back."

"Good. Maybe the doc will give him a shot to shut him up for a while," Jim chuckled. After ordering their drinks, the remaining gunmen sat down at an empty table toward the back of the saloon to wait for Alfredo's return.

Once outside, Alfredo remounted his tired mare and led Jorge's horse to the doctor's house. Alfredo told Jorge to stay in the saddle until he made sure the doctor was available, then dismounted and knocked on Dr. Martin's door.

A few seconds later, a middle-aged woman with white hair answered the door and asked, "May I help you?"

Alfredo explained that his friend had been shot and asked if the doctor was available. The woman nodded and instructed Alfredo to bring the patient into the house. The gunman agreed and trotted back to the horses to help Jorge dismount and guide him into the doctor's house. The white-haired doctor met them a few feet inside the door and pointed toward the examining room.

"Take him to the first room on the left," advised the middle-aged physician. "Let's lay him down on the table. This looks like a gun shot. What happened?"

Alfredo chimed in before Jorge could speak, "On our way to this town, we were bush-wacked. A group of masked men tried to stop us on the road about fifteen miles back. We put spurs to our horses to get away, but my friend here was shot before we got too far. Luckily, we escaped." The doctor was skeptical of this explanation but couldn't prove or disprove the story. In any event, he still had to treat this man.

"I'll need to get the bullet out right away, and your friend seems to be running a fever. He'll have to stay here at least overnight and may not be able to ride again for a week or two."

"Thanks doc. Oh yeah. If you have a minute, can you stitch up my ear too? I think a stray shot caught me. I'll be back in the morning to see how my pal's doing."

Doc Martin readily agreed and deftly stitched Alfredo's earlobe together.

Alfredo left the doc's house after getting his ear repaired, rode back to the saloon and dismounted. Once inside he spotted the rest of his group at a table in the back of the saloon. He sat down in an open chair and gratefully poured himself a drink.

"Well, how did it go?" asked Big Bob.

"The doctor said Jorge would have to spend the night and probably won't be ready to ride for up to two weeks. I told him a lie about being bushwhacked on the road here because he asked how Jorge got shot."

"That's just great!" snarled Jim. "We're not gonna wait a day for Jorge, let alone two weeks. He'll just have to stay here till he's fit and meet us in Denver later."

"I agree," nodded Big Bob. "We're not gonna wait. Alfredo, you go back tomorrow morning and tell Jorge about our plans."

"All right. I'll go before we leave town."

The gang stayed at the saloon for an hour and then decided to find somewhere to eat. Before they left, Rick asked the barkeep if there was a good restaurant nearby and a place they could stay for the night.

The barkeep pointed and advised, "Down on the left you'll find a cantina that serves good Mexican food. Right next door is the hotel."

In the morning, Alfredo returned to the doctor's house and was greeted by the same woman who answered the door the first time. When he asked to see his friend, the lady led him to a room just past the examination room. "He's in here. Your friend is still pretty weak from loss of blood, but he should be okay in a week or two."

Alfredo followed his escort into the room and spotted Jorge, awake and still moaning in pain, propped up against some pillows on a single bed. He asked to speak to his friend privately. Once they were alone, he took a seat on a chair by the edge of the bed and asked, "How are you feeling?"

"How in the hell do you think I feel? It hurts like hell!"

"All right, all right. Jeez, don't have a cow. Listen up. The doctor said you won't be able to travel for a week or two. Jim and Big Bob decided that we can't wait, so they want you to meet us in Denver once you're better."

"Yeah, I expected as much from them. I guess I would have said the same thing. The doc wants to move me over to a hotel, probably today. They have room service for people who need attention. By the way, can I borrow ten dollars till I get to Denver?"

Alfredo laughed and replied, "Do you think I'm a millionaire?" He checked his pockets and came up with twenty dollars. "Just be sure you give this back with your first pay in Denver. Well, I gotta git back. We're leaving shortly."

"Ok, I'll be seeing you soon."

With that, Alfredo rose, waved a hand in farewell and left the doctor's house. Alfredo met up with everyone else at the cantina and sat down at a table beside Rick. Big Bob and Jim were at the next table.

"Well, what's the news?" asked Big Bob.

"Jorge's still hurting and complaining, but at least the bullet's out. He'll be at the doc's until later today, and then they plan to move him over to the hotel to rest. He conned me out of twenty bucks to pay for it."

"I knew you were a sucker, but I guess it couldn't be helped. Hurry up and eat something so we can get on the trail," ordered Big Bob.

In under an hour, the group were mounted and headed north out of town toward Colorado.

At noon the day after Sheriff Anderson's funeral, Tom was cooking pork chops and biscuits for lunch.

"Tom, I know I haven't thanked you enough yet for everything you're doing for me. But I just wanted to tell you now, because I couldn't have done the sale without your help. I'm a little surprised that we got close to forty dollars for everything."

"Well, I think everyone was willing to pay a little more because they felt sorry for what happened to your dad. I'm just glad that everything sold."

"Me too!" Cody chuckled. "I sure didn't want to move that stuff over here or lug it around with me wherever I go."

"Lunch is ready now, so sit down and eat. We have a busy afternoon today. I'm looking forward to seeing how well you shoot."

"I hope you don't expect too much, Tom. That heavy gun will certainly test my accuracy, and my aim isn't that good to begin with." The pair ate in relative silence and left the house to visit the practice range.

"We need to talk to Jeb about borrowing some horses. Our practice area is almost five miles out of town."

"I don't think that'll be a problem. Jeb always let my father and me borrow horses to go fishing."

After obtaining mounts from the stable, Cody and Tom followed the trail west for about five miles, then turned north and rode a short way into the desert to a three-foot deep, five-foot wide gulley.

A variety of cacti grew close to each side that would be ideal shooting targets, including several organ pipes. These can grow nine feet high and have ten or twelve six-inch-wide arms that curve outward from the base, and then rise straight upward. The gulley also sported prickly pears, sagebrush bushes, yucca plants, conifer and mesquite trees, and a rock outcropping on its north side.

They dismounted and tied the horses twenty-five yards away on the south ridge of the gulley to keep them from being spooked by the noise of the gunfire. While Tom determined which cactus would be the best initial target, he and Cody sat on the gulley wall and drank from their canteens.

Once he made his decision, Tom got to his feet and retrieved Cody's practice rig from his saddlebags. Cody buckled the belt and tied down the holster. He then pulled out the pistol and noticed that it had already been filled with ball bullets.

Tom scolded, "When you're checking a gun, Cody, never point it carelessly at anyone. You never know if it's loaded. That's a good way to get yourself or someone else shot. Turn away from everyone whenever you take a revolver from its holster, unless you plan to use it."

"Yeah, I know. My dad told me that, too. I promise to be very careful from now on."

"Good. Now go into the middle of the gulley and target that pipe organ to the right on the top of the north side wall. It's about twenty yards away or so. Try and shoot it about three feet up and in the middle of one of its arms."

"Okay. I hope I can even hit the cactus with this gun."

Cody walked to the middle of the gulley, pulled out the pistol, cocked the hammer, steadied the weapon with two hands and pointed it at the cactus. When he pulled the trigger, the gun jerked upward with a sizable recoil as the bullet left the barrel and yellow, orange and red flames and gray smoke belched from the muzzle. The ball just grazed the left side of one of the cactus arms about three and a half feet up. Not surprisingly, this was not the arm Cody had targeted. Cody turned around and looked ruefully at Tom.

"Well that's not too bad. Did you hit the arm you aimed at?"

"Nope. I aimed at the arm to the right of where the bullet hit."

Tom shook his head and said sarcastically, "Oh great! You won't have the opportunity to bring the pistol up to your eyes in a gunfight, nor will you have time to use both hands."

"Yeah, I guess you're right."

"Now, only use your right hand and aim the same way you just did. You'll have to get used to firing with only one hand. We'll practice this for a week or two, depending on how much your accuracy improves. We'll then switch to your left hand and do the same thing." Cody turned to face the cactus and transferred the gun deliberately to his right hand.

"While aiming, stand sideways to the cactus. Keep your arm straight at eye height. This will give you a little more support as you fire and will also give your opponent a smaller target. Only do this if you have enough time."

Cody turned to the left, pointed his right arm straight out at eye level and pulled the trigger. The bullet missed the cactus entirely. Tom looked over at Cody questioningly.

"I think I missed the whole cactus," admitted Cody sheepishly, as Tom fell back laughing. "This is going to take longer than I thought."

"Don't get down on yourself, boy. It's just going to take some time and practice. Go ahead and fire the rest of the bullets the same way."

Cody fired all four remaining shots in slow succession. He finally hit the correct cactus arm about three feet from the ground on his last attempt. Carefully pointing the gun barrel at the ground, Cody turned toward Tom. "Thank you for stopping me from going after my father's killers. I wouldn't have had a chance against even one of them, let alone the whole gang."

Tom nodded in agreement, "That's right, and you're welcome." Clambering into the gully, Tom set a box of black powder, wads and ball bullets on the ground. He continued, "Let's load you up again and practice for the next ten minutes."

Cody handed the pistol to Tom and watched as the gunsmith loaded the weapon. When the revolver was armed and ready, Cody shot his second six-shot barrage the same way as the first time, hitting the cactus arm only once. He was a little upset with himself but didn't want Tom to see it.

"When I reload the pistol Cody, I want you to watch very carefully." Tom filled a bullet chamber with black powder from a flask, then lightly pushed a wad of paper into the cylinder hole. He then placed the ball on top of the paper and turned the wheel until the cylinder was directly above the loading lever plunger bar, located below the barrel.

He then pulled the lever toward the grip to seat the ball and wad snugly on top of the black powder, and finally greased the end of the chamber. After Tom repeated the process for each load, he placed a firing cap on the round nipple attached to each cylinder. Cody was sure he had learned to load the pistol correctly by watching Tom.

Cody turned his attention back to his target and fired the pistol until it was empty. This time, he hit the arm two times but not in the middle. Cody felt better that at least he'd hit his target twice. They reloaded and fired the revolver three more times before they had to return to town. Cody hit the cactus twice each time and improved to three times on the final round.

Tom seemed pleased that things were progressing, albeit slowly. On the way back to town, he said encouragingly, "Now Cody, don't feel bad about your shooting. Remember, this is the first time you've ever fired a gun one-handed. You'll get better. In the meantime, you'll have to continue practicing your draw every day. We'll come out and shoot again soon."

"That sounds really good to me."

The next two months passed pretty much the same way. Tom and Cody would work their separate jobs and go out at lunch to practice shooting. After work, they'd meet at the house and Cody would practice drawing, cocking and pulling the trigger on his revolver. Cody would work a half day at the livery on Saturdays, then go to the gun shop to practice and help Tom sell guns and bullets. They didn't work on Sundays, but Tom would give Cody advice on his draw.

Over time, Cody's draw speed and shooting accuracy improved. At the gulley, he could usually hit the cactus at least four of every six shots with either hand. Cody was pleased with his progress and had also started repaying Tom for gunpowder and bullets from his earnings at the stable. Tom had to double his order for both each month just to keep up with Cody's lessons.

On the last Saturday in April, Tom decided that Cody was proficient enough to move to the next stage of his training. As they traveled to the gulley after working their half days, Tom announced, "Cody it's time to start drawing your weapon, cocking it and shooting when your upper and lower arm are at a 90° angle." They had to choose a different cactus for target practice because the first one was full of holes and all its arms were sagging toward the ground.

Before he selected a new target, Tom stood by Cody and held his wrist to show him exactly how he should hold the gun. "Cody, I want you to take your time with this shooting exercise. I don't want you to shoot yourself in the foot."

"Okay, I get the idea."

"Now try it slow, so that you get comfortable with the firing position."

Cody tried a slow draw from the holster while pulling back the hammer and bringing the pistol up to the new position. When he fired, he quickly discovered there was significantly more recoil when his arm was bent. It took a dozen shots before Cody even hit the cactus from this new position.

"This is definitely harder, but it'll certainly be faster to shoot someone this way than going all the way to a straight arm shot."

"It certainly will. Most gunfighters use this firing position. Next week, we'll continue practicing with a little more speed. I want you to feel comfortable with this position before we really speed it up. Of course, you can be the fastest gun in the world, but if you can't hit what you are aiming at, then what does it matter?"

"You have a point."

One evening at home after work, Tom began the next phase of Cody's training. "Cody, it's time you start practicing throwing your knife. We'll set up a wide piece of wood behind the house. Just like learning how to use your pistol, you must be proficient throwing your knife accurately with either hand in case one arm is injured. You can practice a half hour each night after work. Once you're done, we'll eat dinner. What do you think of the idea?"

"It sounds reasonable. Let's do it. I want to be ready for any problem that might arise when I start tracking those killers."

From that day onward, Cody practiced throwing his knife both by the handle and by holding it at the very tip of the blade. At the beginning, he wasn't very good, and the knife would frequently bounce off the wooden target without sticking.

It took several weeks of daily practice before the knife stuck in the wood more than occasionally, and even longer to have any success with his left hand. Cody knew it would take a lot more time to become proficient.

Almost two months later, on an otherwise uneventful Wednesday in mid-June, the stage brought a package from the Colt Manufacturing Company to Shiprock's gunsmith. The parcel was wrapped in brown paper secured in place by four string ties.

Tom was glad Cody's guns had finally arrived. He brought the package into the shop's back room and took a folding knife from his pocket to cut the ties. Tom ripped open the wrapping to expose a wooden case containing two matching blue Colt .44s. The beautiful wooden-handled revolvers sat in shallow, felt-lined indentations, one upside down over the other. It was an impressive sight.

Tom carefully removed the bottom pistol and examined it from every angle for manufacturing flaws. He then tested the firing mechanism by half-cocking the hammer and spinning the bullet cylinder. He checked several times, listening with a practiced ear to the loud clicks as each chamber spun past the firing pin.

The noisy clicks meant the revolver was well made and wouldn't jam easily or catch midway between individual bullet chambers. After he was satisfied, he returned the pistol to the case and examined its mate. Both revolvers worked beautifully. Tom made a mental note: *'I really like these guns. I should try to get my customers to purchase more of them.'*

To ensure that the lovely weapons were ready to use, Tom decided to clean and oil them for Cody. It took about an hour, but Tom was very pleased with the results. *'These look great! Cody will be extremely happy.'*

Tom decided to wait until after dinner to surprise him. He rewrapped the pistol case and found the only double-holster belt he had left in stock, since the one he ordered had not yet arrived. Tom took both items to the house before Cody got off work, hid them under his bed and then returned to the shop.

When Cody came to the shop after work, Tom asked conversationally, "Hey, how'd work go today?"

"It was fine. I've been making a lot of horseshoes lately. Jeb said that we have forty now, so I can hold up for a while."

"I guess you're already an expert at something, huh."

"Yeah, I guess so. I wish I could be an expert at other things too," laughed Cody.

"You're doing fine with your training, so don't be discouraged. You've come a long way from where you started. Maybe we'll shake things up a little tomorrow.

"What are you talking about?"

"We'll discuss that after dinner. I'll just clean up for a few minutes and we'll head home."

"It seems like you're hiding something Tom. I hope it's not bad news."

It was Tom's turn to laugh. "Don't be silly, boy. I've picked up some goodies from the Wilsons, that's all. I'm done now, so let's get going."

After he locked up the shop, Tom and Cody headed home.

They finished dinner with a slice of fresh apple pie that Emma Wilson had made that very morning. "When you're done with that pie, Cody, go look under my bed and bring what you find there back to the table."

Cody immediately got excited and exclaimed, "I knew something was up! What is it? I'm not gonna wait," as he leaped from the table and sprinted into Tom's room, dropping quickly to the floor to peer under the bed. He pulled out a wrapped package and a two-holster gun belt and brought them back to the table.

"These must be my new guns. I can't wait to see them!" he exclaimed. Cody swiftly ripped open the wrapping paper and almost reverently placed the box on the table. Coated in wax by the manufacturer, the gun case shimmered gently in the light.

Cody opened the lid and stared silently at the two matching pistols for a minute before he found his voice, "Wow! They're beautiful!" He picked up first one and then the other. "They're so much lighter than the pistol I use now to practice. Tom, do you think these guns will help me draw faster?"

"I think they should make a big difference. Of course, they'll take a while for you to master, especially two at a time."

"I can't wait to try them out!"

"Go ahead and put on the gun belt and rest the revolvers in their holsters. See how the rig feels." Cody was delighted to do exactly what Tom wanted and tried drawing the unloaded weapons several times. "The pistols and gun belt feel great, almost as if they were made just for me!"

"I've already cleaned and oiled them, so why don't you take them off for now? We'll try them out tomorrow afternoon."

"I can't wait!" Cody replied, shaking his head with a big grin on his face. He might even sleep with his new pistols under his pillow tonight.

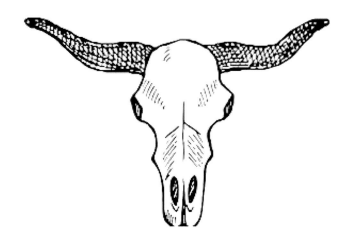

When Tom and Cody arose the next morning, they decided to take the day off from work and spend it at the practice range. They packed two lunches apiece since they were going to be in the desert most of the day. They also brought extra water because the temperature would reach well into the 90s by midday.

When they visited the livery to rent their horses, Cody asked the blacksmith if he could have the day off. Jeb gave Cody his customary employee discount on the rental and his blessing, "Sure Cody. We're all caught up with things around here, thanks to your help at the forge."

Cody wrapped his rig in a bedroll so curious eyes wouldn't spot him wearing a gun belt to the gulley. Gossip spread like wildfire in Shiprock, and

Cody didn't want anyone to realize what he was doing, especially Bill Camp. Bart Camp owned the largest ranch in the area, and Bill was the youngest of his three sons.

A year Cody's senior, Bill was a notorious bully who delighted in harassing Cody and the other boys at school. Bill was the main instigator of the jokes about the sheriff's half-breed son being a poor marksman, and Cody had already fought him to pretty much a draw several times. Cody thought with satisfaction, 'won't *Bill be shocked when I start wearing this rig in town*!'

Once Tom and Cody reached the gulley, Cody eagerly strapped on his new holster. Although Tom had brought along two boxes of ammo, he asked Cody to begin by practicing with unloaded weapons for the next few hours. Tom instructed Cody to first draw and holster his right gun, then his left and finally pull both guns at once.

Cody quickly discovered that these pistols were much easier to draw than his practice gun, although they were snug in their new holsters. Cody knew the fit would loosen up over time but noticed that the front sights were already creating grooves in the leather. This friction of gun against holster would continue to slow his draw in the future.

"Tom, the front sights of these guns are cutting lines into the holsters and making it harder to draw them quickly. Is there anything we can do about that?"

"Yes. If you'd like, we can file down the sights to make them smooth. That way they won't cause any drag when the pistols come out of the holsters."

"I think that would help a lot."

Tom was happy to see Cody's big grin and his excitement over the new rig. As Tom watched the practice, he suggested that Cody slightly bend his knees to shift the holsters a bit toward the ground and make it easier to pull the guns outward, rather than straight up.

Cody practiced his quick draw for over three hours, repeatedly lowering the gun belt to improve his speed. He was pleased that his timing was much faster with the new guns, although his double-draw still felt awkward. Cody realized it would take many more repetitions to master this skill.

"Hey Tom, I've been thinking about something. In addition to filing the sights, can we cut a notch into the front face of the holsters, so the pistols come out more quickly? If we cut a 1½ inch-wide by 2½ inch-long vertical slot on the top each holster, that should increase the draw speed even more."

"Yes, we can do that too, although we don't want to compromise the integrity of the holsters. We must make sure the guns still sit deep enough so that they won't fall out when you're walking or mounting a horse." Cody and Tom washed down their quick lunch with a lot of water because the desert sun was really scorching at the practice range.

After they ate, Tom announced, "Okay Cody, it's time to add something new to your shooting routine. I want you to stand seven feet from the target and complete your normal right, left and combined draw. This is the closest you'll probably be in any confrontation. After we load your guns, you'll fire two bullets from each draw position. Take your time with the first round and try to accurately hit the center of the cactus arm. For the second round, you'll move through the positions, speeding up as much as you can."

"Then you'll fire two careful and two quick shots from each draw position at twenty, forty and sixty feet. These are the most common distances between people in gunfights. I want you to practice this firing routine for the next month."

"Okay, Tom. That sounds pretty cool." Cody drew and fired from seven feet, hitting the cactus twice in the middle with his right hand and once with his left. He then holstered his guns and drew both simultaneously, striking the target again close to center.

"You did well. For the second round, repeat the two-bullet sequence from the same distance, but draw as fast as you can." Cody completed the quick-draw exercise with equal success. "That's good, too. Now follow the same routine for two rounds at twenty, forty and sixty feet."

At twenty feet, Cody struck the correct cactus arm in two of four attempts from each firing position. At forty feet, Cody hit the target twice in twelve tries, once each from the right and left positions. At sixty feet, Cody hit the cactus only once with his right hand.

Tom and Cody repeated this exercise from each distance for two hours. Although Cody had some success at seven and twenty feet, he would need a great deal more practice to be effective at the longer distances. By this point, both Tom and Cody were getting thirsty, so they took a fifteen-minute break.

"Cody, you have enough remaining bullets for one final round of shooting at each distance. Try to complete this as fast as you can. Being somewhat fast and accurate will keep you alive 75% of the time, but if you can become truly fast and remain accurate, it will save your life 100% of the time. Precision shooting develops with lots of practice, so you must practice, practice and practice some more. Keep working on your speed draw at night and whenever you have spare time, and don't forget about your knife throwing."

"Okay Tom, I get the idea. Right now, I'm starting to melt in this heat." Cody fired his remaining bullets as fast as he could at each distance with varying results.

"Cody, let's go home, take a rest and get something to eat."

"I'm all for it. Let's go." Cody unbuckled his rig, rewrapped the gun belt in the bedroll and tied it to the back of his saddle. He and Tom then mounted up and headed home.

Cody continued this routine for a month and gradually became more proficient at all distances in both speed and accuracy. Tom added more shooting positions to Cody's practices, and had him fire not only when standing, but also when kneeling, sitting, and laying on his stomach and back. This new twist added another month to the practice schedule.

Cody was always broke after using his livery stable wages to reimburse Tom for all the ammunition he used, but he didn't want to feel beholden to anyone. Cody's dad had instilled the value of paying his own way into Cody's head at a young age. By repaying Tom every week, he'd be free to leave Shiprock as soon as he was ready to chase down the men that killed his father. Cody felt it wouldn't be long before he would follow their trail.

The next time they went to the gun range, Tom took along a sack of empty food cans for Cody to use as targets. This would be even more challenging due to their smaller size. From now on, Tom wanted Cody to move in a left or right direction when firing his guns because it was harder for an opponent to hit a moving target than a man standing in one place.

He also had Cody practice firing from horseback. The combination of up and down and forward motion of the animal made precision shooting far more difficult. In the beginning, Cody didn't hit anything. After several weeks, he was able to get a few hits from both guns in one movement. Within a month, Cody was hitting more targets.

Little changed in their daily routine during this time. Cody came to the gun shop every day after work and practiced his fast draw. Tom also showed Cody how to break down his revolvers to clean and oil them. According to the gunsmith, this would not only reduce wear and help his pistols last longer but would also ensure that Cody always had fully-functioning weapons. "You always want to have clean and oiled guns when you intend to use them."

Tom also had Cody work on other customers' pistols. He quickly learned the different makes and models of these guns. In case something happened to either one of his own weapons, Tom wanted Cody to be familiar with other guns so that, if necessary, he could find a good replacement.

The final skill Tom wanted Cody to master was shooting at a moving target. To do this, Tom first drilled a hole through one end of a 3-foot long piece of two-by-four. He then hung this contraption from a long nail at the top of a sturdy tripod so that it could swing freely. Finally, Tom attached a four-inch square wooden target to the bottom end of the arm.

Tom would stand by the tripod and release the arm from a high point, then quickly move away so Cody could shoot at the target before it slowed down too much. As always, it took some time for Cody to hit these moving targets comfortably and accurately.

It was late autumn when Cody's seventeenth birthday rolled around on the last day of October, a little more than forty years before the United States would officially start celebrating the popular Halloween holiday. Tom had been pondering for a while what he could get Cody for a birthday present and he figured that a long gun would be a perfect complement to the rest of Cody's arsenal.

A Winchester .44-.40 had arrived last month that Tom had hidden away for this very purpose. After a shot is fired from this lever-action rifle, the shooter pulls a metal oval loop on the bottom which moves downward and forward to eject the spent shell and load a new bullet into the firing chamber. Tom figured Cody would save money because the Winchester took the same caliber ammunition as his pistols.

Not only that, but the rifle had the same powder load, so it would feel similar when fired. Tom decided to treat Cody to a birthday dinner and dessert at Wilson's and then come back to the house for his present. He'd hide the Winchester under his bed, springing it on Cody the same way he did with the pistols.

When Cody came into the shop after work, Tom announced, "Seeing as it's your birthday, we'll take the evening off today and go to Wilson's for dinner."

"Great! Thanks Tom. My mouth is watering already, and my belly is complaining."

Tom laughed, "I bet it is. Let's go."

Tom and Cody had a very satisfying dinner of steak and mashed potatoes with gravy and biscuits. They also each had a slice of the fresh apple pie Emma Wilson made especially for Cody's birthday, and got to take the remainder home with them. They thanked Mrs. Wilson, paid for their meal and headed home.

Once inside, Tom put the remaining dessert in the pie cabinet which also subbed as his storage area for dishes, booze and pots and pans. Like most pie cabinets, Tom's had metal squares in the doors with holes shaped in a design. Cody leaned back in his seat at the table, happily rubbing his full belly. "Thanks for the birthday dinner Tom. I could get used to that every day of the year."

"I'm sure you could, but you won't. I have something for you in my room and I wonder if you know where it might be." With a surprised look, Cody leaped from his chair like a Mexican jumping bean and raced into Tom's room. He checked under the bed and spotted another package. Cody knew what it was the moment he pulled it out and couldn't wait to open it. Cody returned to the table, ripped away the paper and uncovered a new lever-action Winchester rifle.

"Wow! Thanks Tom! It's beautiful. You're going to keep me in servitude until I'm twenty."

Tom laughed and replied, "It's a present, you ninny. You don't have to pay this one back. You've done well over the last nine months and this is a little incentive to continue your education. We'll start practicing with it tomorrow, but we'll have to zero it in first."

True to his word, the next day Tom took Cody several miles past their gun range to a worn path heading south off the main trail. They rode another two miles and stopped by a hill beside a very small butte. Tom and Cody dismounted and tied their horses to a lone Joshua tree on the back side of the hill. They could lay on the hilltop and see for miles to fire at the many cacti dotting the landscape.

Tom pulled the Winchester from the rifle scabbard attached to his saddle, along with a box of .44-.40 cartridges and a pair of binoculars to see hits at longer distances. As they walked up the slope, he advised, "Cody, sometimes there are deer here so if you shoot one, we can bring home some meat."

When they reached the top, Tom studied the vista. There were many large organ pipes scattered about and two lone saguaros between fifty and a hundred yards from their position, ideal for targets. Saguaros have one thick trunk that rises from ten to fifteen feet high with two to four protruding arms that turn skyward at a 90° angle. They resemble someone surrendering when a lawman says, "Hands up."

There was a prickly pear about twenty yards to the left which would be good for zeroing-in the rifle. This process uses a rear sight that can be adjusted both up/down and left/right to ensure that shots hit extremely close to where they are aimed. After Tom fired a few rounds from the rifle, he adjusted the sight upward a few degrees and one degree to the right.

Now it was accurate, at least to the distance of twenty yards. Tom handed the Winchester to Cody and said, "Try and hit the saguaro out about fifty yards to the right. I want you to stand for now. We'll work on other positions over the next few months."

Cody opened the box of bullets and loaded the rifle through the loading gate on its right side.

This "gate" is a small, elongated metal door in front of a spring that helps push it closed after each bullet is inserted. Cody raised the rifle to his shoulder, rested the forward wooden grip area of the barrel in his left hand, aimed at the cactus, fired and missed.

Tom advised Cody to hold the rifle snugly against his shoulder and aim through the back sight to the blade front sight, making sure the top of the back sight was level with the top of the front sight. Cody followed the directions and fired again, hitting the cactus on the left side. Tom said that was better and to told Cody to continue firing until the weapon was empty. Cody fired all seven rounds and hit the cactus three times, but not once in the middle. Cody shot at the same target twenty-one more times with mixed results.

Tom then asked Cody to reload the rifle and aim at the other saguaro a hundred yards away on the left. Tom watched through the binoculars as Cody fired all seven shots, striking the cactus only once on the lower left side.

"Tom, I was aiming at the middle halfway up. Why did the bullet hit so much lower?"

Tom chuckled, "Well, the further away your target, the lower gravity pulls the bullet. You'll have to raise your aim a little to compensate or readjust your sights for longer shots."

"Oh. I didn't know that, but it makes sense." Cody continued shooting at the more distant target, hitting the cactus only four times of twenty-eight tries.

"Well Cody, I see we have a lot of work to do with the Winchester, but we can't ignore your other routines. Your top priority must still be practicing the fast draw with your pistols. How about for every three pistol practices, you'll work on your rifle once and it will be last in the process?"

"Okay, but can we come back here tomorrow to try again with the Winchester? I need to get more experience on the rifle too."

"Sure, Cody. We can return tomorrow and use up another box of ammo. But if you don't do markedly better, then we go back to my proposal."

"Great, let's do it."

The next day after work, they made it to the long-range shooting area in good time. They dismounted, and Tom pulled out the Winchester. Cody grabbed a box of cartridges from his saddlebags and they headed up the slope to the top of the hill. After Tom handed the rifle to Cody, he opened the box of ammo and started placing bullets into the loading gate.

"All right. Aim at the closer saguaro for the first thirty rounds, then use the rest of your shots on the further one. You need to focus first on the nearer target to become more accurate."

"Hopefully, I can do better today than yesterday." Cody began shooting at the closest cactus, hitting it thirteen times of the thirty bullets he shot. Cody fired slowly, taking his time and focusing for a long while between shots. He was happy about this improvement.

"You did pretty well at that distance, but you weren't firing very quickly either. You should be able to shoot faster at fifty yards and slower at the longer distance. Go ahead and shoot at the 100-yard target with the rest of your bullets." Cody only hit this saguaro four times out of twenty shots, but he remembered to sight a little higher and each hit was closer to the midpoint of the cactus.

"The next time we come out, we'll concentrate on only the closer cactus. I want you to shoot more quickly since these men will be most likely be closer and be better shots than you. The faster you can accurately shoot the higher your chances of survival, especially if they are shooting back at you. For now, we'll go back to the gulley and continue practicing moving about while you fire your pistols and improving your accuracy with moving objects."

"All right. I'd rather kill them with my handguns anyway, since they'll be closer and I'll be able to see the fear in their eyes."

It took almost two weeks for the gunmen to make it to the outskirts of Denver. They were amazed by the size of the place. The Colorado Gold Rush had made Denver one of the largest cities in the West. Although new gold and silver strikes would occur over the next sixteen years, only one of those mines is still in operation today.

As they made their way closer to the middle of city, Big Bob and Jim chose a cheap hotel for their base of operations. The plan was for the gang to get hired as guards at the local mines, so Big Bob ordered the men to split up and visit nearby saloons to find out where all the mines were located and whether they were hiring. He knew locals not only met and drank in saloons, but they were perfect places to pick up gossip and find out about almost everything happening around the city.

Most of the mines were west and north of Denver, with only a few to the south and east. They each had many workers mainly digging or panning company claims. The mines that tunneled into the sides of mountains usually worked larger gold deposits. Since Denver didn't have its own mint till 1906, most of Colorado's gold went to the mint in San Francisco to be made into coins and bars.

It took the men a full day to find the locations of all the mines in and around Denver. But none of the customers or barkeeps knew if the mines were hiring. The gang met back at their hotel so that they could talk in private. They didn't want other people around to hear their conversation.

After Big Bob heard what the men discovered, he laid out a plan, "Okay, what I think we should do is that each of us should get hired on at a different big mine. We'll keep our eyes and ears open to learn as much as we can about the mine's operation."

"That way, we may find out exactly when they ship their gold to the city. We can then look for the best areas to ambush shipments and the best times to steal the gold before it gets shipped. I think we should spread these attacks out over time and not draw too much attention to us all at once. What do you all think about this idea?"

Everyone thought Big Bob's idea made a lot of sense. The first step was to hang around the mines and watch who came down to Denver and where they went. Hopefully, several guards from one mine would head for a specific saloon and drink together.

That way, the gang could learn the identities of the guards, determine where they drank and also the places they stayed after they left the saloon. It took about two weeks for the gang to ferret out the guards' schedules.

Once they learned the routine, all four gang members went to one of the saloons visited by the guards. Then they'd follow, abduct and murder a guard after he'd been drinking, dumping the body late at night. The gang made these kills with knives, because they were quieter and were less likely to draw attention.

The next day, one of the killers would visit that specific mine about an hour after starting time and ask about a job. By then, the mine owners were aware that the guard didn't show up for work. If the gunman wasn't hired, he'd leave his name and where he was staying in case a position came open.

Two days later, he'd return to the mine and, low and behold, get hired on the spot. This strategy worked well, and soon all four men had jobs as guards at four different mines. They would add a fifth mine after Jorge arrived, which they hoped would be soon.

It took the full two weeks for Jorge to feel well enough to travel. His shoulder was still sore, but his wound had healed around the stitches. Dr. Martin had visited him once at the hotel early on, and Jorge had returned twice for appointments at the office.

Today was his last visit to the doctor to get the stiches removed. Jorge had paid one of the hotel staff go to the stable, get his mount saddled and ready to ride, then bring the horse back to the hotel. Jorge paid his hotel bill and rode over to Dr. Martin's house. It didn't take long to remove the stitches, and he was mounted and headed on the trail northward in under ten minutes.

It took Jorge the same amount of time it took the others to reach Denver. By the time he arrived, the rest of the bunch had been working at their own mines for about three weeks. Big Bob chose a mine for Jorge, and another guard was found murdered. These killings were perplexing to the local police force because there were no suspects and no witnesses.

The gunmen worked at their jobs for almost nine months before Big Bob believed they had acquired enough information about the schedule of gold shipments and mine operations to take the next step. Since they were well-paid, the gang could afford to relocate to a boarding house centrally located between their jobs at the mines, and even closer to the middle of the city. This made the gunmen appear more prosperous and involved within the community, and less like transients who might be planning something sinister.

It took the gang another month to plan their first heist. They were going to start with Rick's mine, as his employer seemed to have the loosest security when it shipped gold to its bank in Denver. Big Bob decided that everyone except Rick would take the day off and would all dress in tan clothes, hats and handkerchiefs to cover their faces, purchased from five different stores in the city.

Rick would position himself as one of two guards riding at the back of the security procession. There were two additional guards riding in front, and a driver and two men sitting inside the buckboard carrying the shipment. It was about ten miles from the mine to the bank in Denver.

There were several places the gang could ambush the gold transport, but they wanted somewhere they could attack the guards in a crossfire from both sides at once. This narrowed the options to one place with rock outcroppings on both sides of the trail about mid-trip between the mine and the bank.

The gang would wait in hiding on the outcrops until the buckboard was right next to them. Once the shots began, Rick would kill the guard riding next to him and then concentrate on the men in the buckboard. Two of the hidden shooters would hit the front riders, and the other two would hit the men in the back of the buckboard and the driver.

Once all the mine employees were dead, one of the killers would drive the buckboard, two would ride horses in front and two would ride horses in back. They planned to travel down the main road for another mile, then turn off the trail and go a short distance to bury the gold. The bandits would then drive the buckboard back to the ambush spot, erasing the wagon wheel tracks between the gold cache and the ambush site. Rick would then race back to the mine to report the hijacking.

Rick was not completely sober when he showed up for work the next day. Two large men carried the heavy lock box, generally used on stagecoaches, and heaved it into the back of the buckboard. Two guards armed with double-barreled shotguns then climbed into the back of the buckboard and the four other guards mounted their horses.

The day was cloudy, and folks thought it might rain later. The shipment left the mine around 10:30 in the morning, and the mine manager warned the guards to be careful on their hour-long journey. Although there hadn't been any robberies yet, there was always a first time. Rick thought to himself, '*I wonder if the manager is psychic?*'

It would take about thirty minutes for the shipment to reach the gunmen already waiting at the ambush site. They had tethered their horses some ways off, so that they wouldn't make noise to alert the guards. "All right, men, let's review. Jim and I will be on the right side of the trail, thirty yards past where you two will be hiding on the left. We'll use our rifles during the attack. Don't miss with your first shots. We can't afford any of the guards breaking away and alerting anyone."

"Jim and I will start by shooting the lead riders. You two shoot the buckboard guards and driver after we start firing. We'll grab the two lead horses and Rick will get the other guard's horse in back. The shipment should be here in about fifteen minutes. Does everyone understand the plan I laid out?" asked Big Bob. Everyone nodded and took their positions.

Well, the robbery worked just the way they planned with no one the wiser. Big Bob and Jim began firing as the lead riders were eighteen yards past Alfredo and Jorge. Big Bob hit the left front guard in mid-chest, blood spewing from the hole in a misty scarlet spray. The guard was flung sideways from his horse, dropping his rifle.

Jim hit the other front guard in the right side of his throat, cherry red blood spraying from the hole on the left where the bullet exited. The man brought his hands together to his throat, also dropping his rifle. Jim had to shoot him again, this time in the middle of his chest. He, too, toppled from his mount.

The guards in the buckboard were now kneeling, moving their shotguns back and forth and looking in all directions to try and spot the shooters. Alfredo hit one guard in his left side just under the armpit. The shot must have found his heart because a burgundy stream poured out of the wound.

As he fell, the man's finger pulled the shotgun trigger, sending pellets harmlessly into the bushes by the trail. His lifeless body fell back into the buckboard. Jorge hit the other guard in the left side of the head, crimson blood and bits of brain matter flying to the right with the bullet. He slumped dead over the edge of the buckboard.

Once Rick heard the first shots, he turned toward the guard beside him, pulled out his handgun and shot the man three times in quick succession. The guard was hit in the chest and left side and thrown from his horse, along with his rifle. Bright red blood stained his shirt where the bullets struck.

The buckboard driver didn't stop once the shooting started. Instead, he whipped the two-horse team into a gallop to try to escape. Unfortunately, he, too, didn't live long. He was only fifteen feet from the gunmen when both Big Bob and Jim fired at him simultaneously.

The driver was hit on both sides of his chest, one bullet puncturing his right lung and the other hitting his heart. The man flew backwards from his seat into the back of the buckboard, his feet sticking up into the air over the seat.

"Rick, go grab the reins and stop the buckboard team!" yelled Big Bob.

"Okay," Rick hollered, spurring his mount to catch the runaway buckboard. It took him a minute or two to reach the frightened horses and bring them to a stop. Rick waited with team until his partners reached him.

In the meantime, the other gunmen scrambled from their hiding places and stepped onto the trail. They made sure the fallen guards were dead, then rifled their pockets to steal their money and valuables. Then Alfredo retrieved the three guards' horses and pulled Jorge up behind him. Once Big Bob and Jim were mounted, the gang rode down the trail to catch up with Rick.

Rick was still holding the team when the others arrived. Big Bob ordered, "Jorge and Alfredo, dump the bodies out of the buckboard. We don't want them there if we meet someone as we go to hide the gold. We still have a mile before the turnoff to our hiding place."

"So far, we've been lucky. Let's get into our places. Jorge, you drive the buckboard. Jim and I will be in the lead. Rick and Alfredo, you take the back. Keep your eyes open and let's get going."

It took the gang a few minutes to get to the turnoff. Jorge turned the buckboard left and urged the team down a rutted old road to a closed mine. The gunmen dug a hole behind a large boulder to the right of the entrance, then used a rifle butt to bust the padlock on the lock box. Inside were fifteen long, slender bags containing slightly more than $35,000 in gold from the heist.

Jorge took the buckboard and the others rode the mine's horses back to the ambush spot, carefully covering their tracks. They abandoned the horses and buckboard there, then hiked back to their own mounts.

Rick rode madly back to the mine only after his partners were well on their way to the boarding house. His story would have to be believable, so that the mine owners wouldn't suspect him. Rick eventually rode back to the ambush spot with the mine manager and ten other armed men, but of course, it was too late. Everyone was dead, and the gold was gone.

Big Bob's gang waited three months before their next heist. They had to plan this one more carefully and would have to wait at least this long between each of the other robberies. They decided to choose a mine located in a different direction from Denver. Since their first robbery was north of the city, they would hit to the south next, then west, east and finally north again.

Unfortunately for Rick, the gang hit only one more shipment before they decided to let him go. He had begun to drink too much, and the others were worried that he might let information spill when he was drinking.

Naturally, Rick was pissed about the situation, but he wasn't as fast a draw as most of the other men. The group decided to let him leave with one bag of gold worth a little over $2,000 as compensation. Rick left Denver and headed back to Arizona.

One thing Cody did every day at work was to watch the people passing by the livery and the gun shop. He hoped to spot the faces of the men that murdered his father, but so far, no one matched what he remembered. The next seven months were a tedious repetition of work and practice.

Cody was tired of all this training and was increasingly eager to go after his dad's murderers. After all, Tom said that he had become very fast with his quick draw and it seemed to Cody that he was now much faster than his father ever was.

Once Tom notched grooves into the front face of his holsters, Cody could pull his pistols more quickly. This reduced his draw time a half to as much as a full second less than an opponent drawing from an unmodified holster.

Although Tom thought that Cody was probably faster now than any of the men who killed his dad, he wanted the boy to continue practicing for a few more months to increase his speed even more. Tom had begun throwing pairs of silver dollars into the air as targets for Cody. He wanted to make sure Cody could hit them both before they struck the ground. To Tom, this would indicate that his pupil was nearing the end of his training and could hit just about anything he shot at with great accuracy and speed.

Late summer had arrived again when Cody began openly wearing his gun belt most of the time. People in town were surprised because they believed he was still a novice shooter of one gun, let alone two. Cody's schoolmates had long since spread the word around town that he wasn't very good with guns. Little did the locals know that he was already one of the fastest guns in the West and would only get better with time and practice.

Cody's nemesis, Bill, had come into town with his family to pick up supplies from the general store and eat at Wilson's while they were in town. It was close to lunch time when Bill spotted Cody walking from the stable to Tom's wearing his guns. Bill looked at his brothers and said, "Look at Cody strutting around like a gun-slinging dandy. I'm going to go over and kid him some more. That half-breed is the worst shot in the county. Maybe I can scare him a little in the process."

Bill's older brothers snickered and encouraged him to go ahead. They'd watch from a distance. Bill dismounted from his horse and approached Cody, trying to cut him off before he got to the gun shop.

Cody saw Bill striding toward him smirking maliciously and thought to himself, 'Oh great! Why is that pest headed my way?'

"Hey Cody, where are you going?"

"I'm headed to the gun shop." Cody tried to ignore the bully, but Bill blocked his path.

"You should have stuck to a bow and arrow, Injun boy. Wearing a gun belt is probably the worst idea you ever had. We all know you shoot like a girl. Guns are for real men. You'd better take them off before you get yourself killed."

"Leave me alone, will you? I have things to do for Tom and I don't have time for you and your foolishness."

Bill didn't like Cody's tone and began to get ticked-off. He started to reach for the pistol in

Cody's right holster. Cody saw his move, smacked Bill's hand away easily and shoved the bully back a foot or two.

"Don't ever try to take my guns again!" he exclaimed sternly. "Why don't you just go back to your family? Get away from me!"

By this time, Tom and a customer from one of the ranches were watching the confrontation from inside the shop. Tom didn't like what was happening, excused himself from the counter and opened the front door. Trying to defuse a possibly nasty encounter, Tom asked, "Cody, can you please come in here?"

Cody had turned slightly to his left to comply with Tom's request when he saw Bill barreling toward him again. By now, his work at the livery stable had put a lot of hard muscle on Cody's growing frame. Bill didn't seem to recognize this fact as he physically attacked, swinging his right fist at Cody's head. Cody moved his head out of the way and grabbed Bill's arm and shoulder, using the bully's own momentum to shove him into the street. Bill stumbled a few steps before he regained his balance.

"Nobody pushes me around, especially you, you greenhorn."

Turning to face Bill, Cody snarled, "Leave me alone or you'll regret it."

Bill's brothers had dismounted and were closing the gap between themselves and the altercation. At this point, they weren't going to come to their brother's aid because they thought that Bill could take care of this guy. Both Cody and Tom noticed their approach, and Tom stepped into the street.

"Okay Cody, I guess you need to be shown who is boss in this town. Let's go at it right now."

Sighing, Cody replied, "If that'll get you to go away faster, it's fine by me." Cody removed his gun belt and handed it to Tom. "Please don't get involved, Tom. I hope this won't be more than a fist fight. Even if I lose, maybe he'll just go away."

Tom whispered softly so no one else could hear, "Just do your best and kick his butt."

Bill had also removed his gun belt, handing it to his oldest brother Mark and ordering his family to stay out of the fight. They agreed, and Bill stomped angrily toward Cody. By now, many locals had crowded around to see the action. Fist fights in Shiprock were always a good form of entertainment, so long as they didn't lead to something deadly.

Cody and Bill started circling and moving closer to each other. Bill lunged forward and aimed another right hook at Cody's head. Cody dodged to his left, pushing Bill away. Bill turned quickly and raced back toward Cody, this time attempting to grapple with him. He wanted to get Cody on the ground before throwing another punch.

Cody met his charge but was not unbalanced enough to fall. Instead, he twisted his body to the left, grabbed Bill around the upper torso and threw him three feet into the air. Bill landed hard on his left side and rolled over, fuming mad now.

Unluckily for Bill, he was unaware that Tom had been instructing Cody in both wrestling and boxing over the last two years. Since he had gotten so strong from working at Jed's, Cody usually won at wrestling, but Tom still had the upper hand in boxing.

Bill came flying back and made a full body jump onto his opponent. This time, they both hit the ground and rolled in the dusty sand before either one started throwing punches. Bill began by hitting Cody weakly in the stomach with his left fist, while throwing a right at Cody's head.

Cody ignored the punch to his stomach, blocked Bill's right with his left forearm and then connected with a powerful right of his own to Bill's left cheek, just under the eye. The blow knocked Bill back onto the ground on his right side. Cody rose slowly into a crouching stance, waiting for Bill to get back to his feet.

"Have you had enough yet Bill?"

"The hell I have! We've just begun, and you'll be sorry." Bill rose to his feet and marched back toward Cody. Bill's brothers were goading him to take care of this guy, hooting and hollering. Bill's face was getting red, not only from Cody's blow but his own growing anger.

Bill began throwing numerous punches at Cody's head and body. Cody blocked most of them, except one that hit him along the right side of his nose. Blood started to flow, but Cody ignored it. Cody blocked another left aimed at his head and threw a left hook of his own to the right side of Bill's face, followed by a quick right to his stomach that doubled Bill over and drove out his breath in a loud "oomph."

Cody then grabbed Bill's hair, pulled up his head and used all his own strength and body weight to plant a powerful right to the bully's jaw. Bill's head snapped to the right and his unconscious body fell to the ground a few feet away. Cody straightened up slowly, using his left shirt sleeve to wipe the ruby droplets dripping from his nose.

Bill remained motionless in the dirt on his back. Glaring at Cody, his brothers hurried over and hefted Bill from the ground, then dragged him between them to the family buckboard. Cody watched them retreat, then turned toward a smiling Tom.

"You did pretty good there, Cody. I'd watch out for Bill in the future though. He'll probably want retribution for the licking you gave him and will most likely come after you with his guns."

"That would be the most serious mistake of his life Tom, but then again, Bill was never the smartest kid in school. If he comes gunning for me, I'm sure his brothers will accompany him. I might have to leave town sooner than we agreed."

"Hopefully, this whole thing will blow over and not result in further senseless violence. But, you may have a point. All those boys are hard-nosed and bad tempered, just like their daddy. You'd better watch for his brothers, too."

"Gee, willikers, I don't need this kind of trouble. Why couldn't Bill just mind his own business?"

"At this point, that's water under the bridge. Just be vigilant for the next few weeks and stay away from school for now. Come into the shop and we'll fix up your face."

Before heading inside, Tom paused to glance at the Camp buckboard. Bill's parents waited on the wagon's front bench until he was loaded by his brothers into the back, then immediately turned the buckboard around and headed west out of town toward their ranch. '*I guess they figured they'd better git before anything else happened.*' As Tom turned toward the shop, he saw his customer leave. The ranch hand waved a farewell and announced that he'd return later.

Cody was waiting in the back room when Tom entered the shop. The gunsmith fetched a cloth, dunked it into a bucket of water and wrung it out a little. Tom then handed it to Cody and advised him to wipe the blood from his face. By this time, the blood had stopped flowing from Cody's left nostril. His nose hurt some, but otherwise he was okay.

"I thought the fight might have gone on longer, but you certainly got in one good lick to stop it in a hurry."

"Yeah, I thought it was going to go on for a while too. I got lucky with one good punch. I'm just worried now that once Bill wakes up, he'll be coming for me."

"I think his father will tell him to wait a spell before coming back into town. I don't think you have anything to worry about for a while, but you never know." Cody and Tom worked in the shop for the rest of the day and headed home at closing time for an uneventful evening.

The next day, Cody was working at Jeb's when a stagecoach came into town from the east. As always, he checked each of the people that arrived to see if any of the men that murdered his father had returned to town.

The stage stopped in front of the saloon every time it came into Shiprock. This way, travelers could get out, stretch their legs and get something strong from the saloon to wash the dust out of their throats. Most men that left the stagecoach went directly into the saloon. People not inclined to drink could walk down to Wilson's restaurant for food and water.

This time, a woman wearing a very frilly, long white dress with a red flowery pattern and a short scarlet jacket stepped off the stage and went into the saloon. Since he didn't see her face, Cody wasn't sure how old she was, but he wasn't used to women of any age going into the saloon, especially by themselves. This piqued his interest and he decided to stroll over and look inside the saloon to get a closer look at the lady. He yelled to Jeb, "I'm going over to the saloon for a minute."

"Okay, but I don't want to smell drink on you when you return. We still have a few things to do before we quit today."

"All right, I won't drink, Jeb." Cody strapped on his gun belt, just in case.

Cody had only been in the saloon with Tom a few times. Whenever he accompanied Tom, Cody would search all the patrons' faces for his dad's murderers. Last month, Tom let him have a shot of whiskey, which burned his throat as it went into his belly.

Cody didn't particularly like it, but he figured whiskey was probably an acquired taste. Cody wasn't particularly fond of beer either. Tom was happy the boy hadn't yet learned to enjoy drinking any kind of alcohol, as too much liquor confuses the mind and slows the reflexes.

Cody stopped at the swinging doors and peeked inside the saloon. Most of the customers were standing at the bar either drinking or waiting for their drinks to be poured. The woman was seated facing the saloon doors at a back table and sipping a large shot of whiskey. She was watching everyone and noticed Cody peering over the doors from outside.

Cody decided to enter the saloon and have a good look at the men at the bar. Perhaps he'd also get a chance to get a better look at the woman. Cody moseyed toward the nearest end of the bar to observe the first three men leaning against the counter. He determined that none of them were the killers. He then moved slowly around the room to reach the far end of the bar.

Cody glanced quickly at the woman and noticed that she didn't seem much older than himself. He didn't stop to say hello, however - he still had spying on his mind.

Cody planted himself at this end of the bar and carefully studied the last two customers. They didn't look familiar either. Frank glanced his way and Cody subtly shook his head. Frank knew that Cody habitually searched for his dad's killers among the people who came into the saloon for a drink.

The woman at the table kept her eyes on the young man from the moment he entered the saloon. She had an idea why he looked so carefully at all the bar patrons. For some reason, he must be searching for someone or perhaps more than one person. Cody had finished checking the customers and glanced again in the woman's direction as he moved toward the saloon doors.

To his surprise, she motioned to him and said, "Hey you, come over here a minute."

Cody stopped walking and turned toward her. "Are you talking to me, miss?"

"Yes."

Cody walked nervously over to her table and stopped across from the lady. He was still rather shy about talking to women.

"Have a seat for a while, stranger." Cody pulled out the chair in front of him and quickly sat down. "Do you want something to drink?"

"No thanks. I need to get back to work in a little while. What can I do for you?" From this distance, Cody noticed that the lady was pretty.

She had light brown hair that hung down to her shoulders in large ringlets. Her eyes were hazel green, she had a small, cute, button nose and large, wide, red lips.

Her cream-colored dress was sprinkled with small red roses and had long sleeves that ended in lace cuffs. It also had lace starting at the shoulder and going up the lady's neck to the bottom of her chin. She watched Cody look her over and gave him a small smile.

"I noticed that you studied all the men that came into the saloon. Are you looking for someone in particular?"

"Yes, I'm looking for five different men. I was hoping that at least one of them was on the stage."

"Why are you looking for them?"

"They came through town over a year ago. While they were in the saloon, they killed my father who was the sheriff."

"I'm sorry to hear that. So, are you looking to take revenge on these men?"

"You could say that, but I look at it more as retribution."

"My name is Rachel. What's yours?" Cody told her his name and wondered why she was curious about him.

"You look like someone I knew a few years ago. I thought you might be him."

"Are you continuing on the stage to your destination?"

"I might stay in town a short while to rest until the next stage goes West."

"There's a nice hotel with a restaurant that serves very good food just down the street. Do you have a husband or job where you're going?"

Rachel laughed and replied, "No, neither one of those things. I wanted to see the West and have an adventure."

Cody thought a minute before responding, "You're a brave woman to travel alone. Your family must be rich for you to be traveling."

"No, I don't have any family any more. I saved some money from my last job is all," Rachel smiled.

"Are you a school teacher or bank clerk?"

Rachel thought, '*this is probably a sweet kid with no real-world experience.*' She smiled again and replied, "No, Cody, nothing so noble. I was a saloon girl who was paid to entice men to drink more in the establishment I worked at."

Cody was a little shocked and raised his eyes, thinking she was too young and seemingly too refined to work in a saloon. "Oh. Okay. Since you're thinking of staying in town for a while, are you going to work for Frank?"

"We are in negotiations right now. He is thinking about how much he's willing to pay me."

"Well, I hope you do stay because I'd like to talk to you again. But, right now, I really do need to get back to work. When you go to the hotel, tell Mrs. Wilson I sent you and she may give you a break on lodging."

"Thank you. I'll do that," Rachel replied, giving Cody a wink.

As he pushed back his chair and rose from the table, Cody added, "Okay, great. I'll see you later."

Cody had turned away and begun heading toward the doors when he heard Rachel reply, "See you later."

Twenty minutes after he left, Cody returned to the stable. Jeb understood why Cody visited the saloon or stood by the stagecoach when new people arrived in town. He and Tom had spoken about Cody's repeated searches for his father's killers and agreed to inform one another as quickly as possible if Cody ever found one of the men. Hopefully, they'd be able to have his back, assuming the full pack of gunmen didn't return at once.

Shiprock had been without a sheriff since Richard had been killed. The town was still looking and had even sent a letter to the State a year ago about an appointment. So far, they hadn't heard anything back. The locals just assumed that the town was too small to warrant the permanent posting of a U.S. marshal or deputy marshal.

About five months ago, a U.S. marshal and deputy did come through Shiprock on the trail of some cattle rustlers that were plaguing northwest New Mexico. Neither of them had heard about the town's request and they doubted that the State would bother to reply. They promised to keep their ears open about anyone willing to take on the sheriff's job but cautioned that it might take a fair amount of time.

Tom was given the unofficial title of "local constable" since he had been the marshal of

Taos, New Mexico almost thirty years earlier. Of course, he was nowhere near as fast on the draw now as he was back then in his twenties. Age had taken its inevitable toll on both Tom's speed and muscle tone.

If something serious ever happened around Shiprock, Tom planned to bring Cody along to help him resolve the problem. Tom hadn't yet mentioned this to Cody and the gunsmith hoped that he would never need to.

Although Cody had been practicing for nearly two years, Tom still wasn't sure how he'd act in an actual showdown. *'I know that Cody can now outdraw almost anyone and I'm pretty sure the boy has the courage to kill another man, but when push comes to shove, you just never know how folks are going to react. It's only natural to be scared for one's own life. Of course, if Cody ever faces one of the skunks that murdered his dad, his rage will take over and I believe he'd rather die trying to get his revenge than live with backing down from that gunfight.'*

On occasion, Tom had seen Cody's anger about his father's murder flare during practice sessions. But he also knew from personal experience that Cody would certainly be scared in a gunfight. Tom remembered how terrified he'd been the first time he'd squared off against a bad gunman. Luckily, he was a little faster than the man he faced. Tom could still recall his dry mouth, how his body shook for some time after the incident and his tremendous feeling of relief to have survived.

Over the next month, Cody began spending more evening hours visiting Rachel at the saloon. Tom accompanied him sometimes after work to keep a watchful eye on the youngster. The gunsmith hoped that this was just a blooming friendship but feared that Cody was becoming smitten with Rachel.

Although he had danced with various schoolmates at the local dances, Cody had never been seriously involved with any of the town girls. Since his father died, Cody had been too busy training to devote much thought to girls. He hadn't even seemed interested until now, but that could change at any time and Tom suspected that it would, sooner rather than later.

Tom worried that Rachel might be leading Cody on, but the gunsmith believed the pretty saloon girl really did like him. Unfortunately, Tom could see that Cody was bothered when Rachel sat and drank with other men while working for Frank.

Sometimes, after waiting a while for Rachel to come over to his table, Cody would storm out of the saloon when she stayed what he considered too long with other men. Aware that Cody was becoming a little jealous, Rachel advised him that she wasn't interested in starting a serious relationship with anyone right now. This also didn't sit well with Cody, but there was nothing he could do about it.

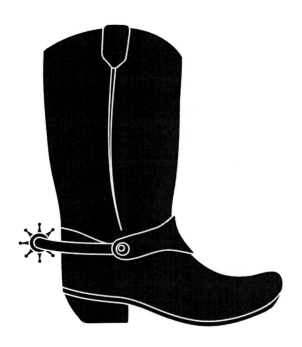

It was early December when a single rider came down Main Street. He rode up to the saloon, dismounted and went inside. Tom had been putting a new pistol into one of the gun cases when he noticed the fellow. He didn't think anything of it, since lots of single riders had come and gone through Shiprock over the last few years.

What he didn't know was that this man was Rick, one of the gunmen that shot Cody's father. Today would turn out to be a defining moment in Cody's life.

Evidently, Rick didn't remember Shiprock since the gang were only in it for an hour or so years ago and he'd been pretty drunk at the time. In the two years since they left the sheriff dead on the saloon floor, the gang had visited countless other settlements. Rick barely remembered any of them except the big cities. He'd been to Silver City, Leadville and Denver and was now headed back toward Tucson and Phoenix, Arizona.

By the time he left Denver, Rick was sick of being bossed around. At first, he liked working as a guard and then stealing gold from some of the biggest mines in Colorado. The money was good, but he had a falling out with the gang after showing up to a heist drunk after being out late the night before.

Big Bob warned him if he showed up drunk one more time, he was through. Well, it wasn't too long before it happened again, and he and the gang parted ways. Rick left Denver and was heading back to more familiar places.

Inside the saloon, Rick bellied up to the bar and called for a bottle of whiskey and a glass. Frank strolled over, poured him a drink, placed the bottle on the bar and mechanically asked for payment without even glancing at the stranger.

When Frank picked up the money Rick threw onto the bar, he finally took a cursory look at his new customer. The barkeep was shocked to recognize the face of one of the men that killed Sheriff Anderson in the only gunfight that had ever occurred in his saloon. Frank quickly turned away, so the man wouldn't see his surprised expression.

Frank knew he had to rush the news to Tom at the gun shop and scanned the room for a messenger. The only person he saw was Rachel at her usual table against the back wall. By this time, Rick and his bottle were settled at a table near the front of the saloon. Frank motioned for Rachel to join him at the end of the bar.

Frank had Rachel lean close to him and whispered, "I need you to go over to Tom's gun shop for me. Tell him that one of the men who shot the sheriff came back to town and is drinking over at that table near the front."

Rachel looked a little alarmed since she knew what this would mean for Cody. "Okay Frank, I hoped this day would never come. I feel something bad is about to happen."

"Yeah, I know how you feel, but it's not up to us to make that decision. Hurry up, but don't make it look like you're running out of here. Just casually walk out and try not to be afraid."

As Rachel strolled past the man sitting at the table, he looked up, smiled and patted his knee. "Hey missy, how about you come over and sit with me a while?"

"I'll be right back good lookin' so don't you go anywhere," replied Rachel, forcing a smile.

"Don't take too long because I'll be waiting for you."

Rachel nodded her head at the gunman and walked nonchalantly through the swinging doors of the saloon. Once outside, Rachel scurried across the street to Tom's and rushed into the shop. Tom was cleaning the glass top of one of the display cabinets when she arrived.

"Tom, there is a stranger drinking at the saloon at a table near the front that Frank recognized as one of the men that killed Cody's father," Rachel blurted excitedly, "and he wants me to sit with him. What should I do?"

Tom instantly straightened up and stared at the girl, looking surprised and a little frightened. "What!" As Rachel repeated the message, Tom strode out from behind the counter.

"Rachel, this is very important. I want you to return to the saloon, tell Frank I understand

and ask him to keep a watchful eye on the man. If you think you can sit with the fellow without being too scared, that would help a lot."

"I'll try, Tom."

"All right. Now head back to the saloon and try not to be nervous if you can help it."

Even before Rachel reached the swinging doors of the saloon, Tom had left his shop and was hurrying down the street to the livery stable. As he entered, Tom spied Cody working in the back and waved to him before striding into Jeb's office and shutting the door. Jeb was seated at his desk doing paperwork.

"Jeb, the day we feared has arrived. It's possible that one of the men that killed Cody's father is in the saloon."

Jumping straight out of his chair Jeb whispered hoarsely, "Are you sure?" Tom repeated Frank's message.

"Jeb, you saw all the gunmen, too. Why don't you go over to the saloon and purchase a tankard of beer, making sure you get a good look at the man sitting at the table near the door? Then, bring it back here and let me know what you think." Jeb was concerned and a little unsettled.

He agreed to visit the saloon and try to verify Frank's identification.

"One more thing, Jeb. Let's not tell Cody until we're sure this is one of the gunmen." Jeb nodded in agreement and hastily trotted out of the livery stable toward the saloon.

Tom left the office and walked over to Cody, who was restacking some bales of hay. Cody was a little curious that Tom would visit Jeb in the middle of the day.

"Hey Tom, what brings you down here at this time of day?"

Thinking quickly on his feet, Tom replied, "I told Jeb that we weren't going to need the horses today. I am feeling a little tired and want to take some time off to rest."

"Oh. I had no idea that you were feeling poorly."

"No, nothing like that. I'm just a little tired is all."

"Where'd Jeb go?"

Tom replied with a little white lie, "I'm not sure, but he said he'd be right back. How are things going here?"

"Good. Jeb said we're going to work on a new wheel for the McDonald's buckboard. He said that he'd teach me how to put the wheel together, as well as put the metal stripping around the outside."

"Wow, you are certainly learning a lot of useful stuff that will help you in the future."

"I guess so." Tom and Cody exchanged some good-natured banter as they waited for Jeb to return.

As Jeb hurried toward the saloon, he decided to look over the doors first to see who else might be inside. He paused for a second at the doorway but could only see the empty area by the bar. He then pushed open the right swinging door and peered around the room as he entered.

Jeb saw Frank at the farthest end of the bar polishing the wooden top. The barkeep gave Jeb a meaningful look and nodded slightly toward the front. Jeb glanced to his right and noticed Rachel sitting with a man. He couldn't see the guy's face, so he kept moving toward Frank.

"Hey Frank, can you get me a small cask of beer for me and Tom to split?"

"Sure thing, Jeb." Frank continued softly, "The guy is over there with Rachel. Why don't you meander over and say howdy to Rachel? He'll most likely look up at you then."

"That's a good idea. I'll be back in a minute for the cask."

Approaching the table where Rachel and the man were seated, Jeb declared, "Hi Rachel. Are you going to be around later today?"

"Hi Jeb. Sure, I'll be around till about seven o'clock tonight."

Jeb got a good look at Rachel's companion. He was definitely one of the men that killed the sheriff. Jeb continued, "Okay, see you then." He nodded at the man, then turned away from the table and sauntered back toward the bar.

"See yah," replied Rachel.

Jeb leaned on the bar and waited for Frank to return with the beer. Frank finally came back with the small cask and set it down in front of Jeb.

"Yup, that's surely one of the men from the gunfight. I'm going to return to my place and talk to Tom. My guess is that we'll formulate some plan to lure him out of your saloon and give Cody a chance at retribution."

"Sounds pretty good to me. I just don't want it to happen in here again."

Jeb picked up the small cask and headed out of the saloon, making sure not to look directly at the table where the gunman sat. He noticed out of the corner of his eye that the gunman watched him leave. Jeb wasn't sure if the fellow recognized him, but he hoped not. Jeb walked even faster back to the stable than he did coming to the saloon.

Jeb saw Tom talking to Cody as he neared the stable. He walked toward them, nodding as he approached. Tom understood immediately but waited for Jeb to speak. Jeb announced, "Yup, that's one of the gunmen."

"What are you two talking about?" asked Cody looking back and forth between Tom and Jeb.

Tom replied calmly, "Cody, the day has finally come. One of the men that killed your father is in town, drinking at the saloon." Shocked by the news, Cody began blindly trotting out of the stable.

Before he'd gone more than a few steps, Tom grabbed his left arm to stop him, "Wait a minute

Cody. Let's talk a few minutes about what we want to do."

Cody shrugged off the gunsmith's hand and replied angrily, "Don't try to stop me, Tom."

Despite his protest, Jeb jumped in front of Cody, blocking his path. "Cody, just a minute. The guy is sitting in the saloon with Rachel. You don't want to endanger her or possibly even get her killed in any gunplay, do you?"

The thought stopped Cody in his tracks. He took a deep breath, turned around and moved to the peg where he'd hung his gun belt. He was so fired up he'd almost forgotten about his guns. Tom and Jeb followed, talking to each other.

"Jeb, you said he's with Rachel right now, correct?"

"Yes, Tom. They're at a table on the right side of the saloon, just inside the door."

Cody slung his gun belt around his body, made sure it was snug and leaned over to fasten the holsters' leather tie-downs to his legs. Once he finished, he stood up and pushed the belt down to its usual position.

"Okay. What we might want to try is for Cody to go into the saloon and confront Rachel, maybe accusing her of stepping out on him. Hopefully, she'll catch on quickly and get away from the table," suggested Tom.

"That should work. Cody, you'll want to check the guy out too. See if you recognize him yourself," added Jeb.

"Once you recognize him, tell him that you know he's one of the men that murdered your father two years ago. Announce that you're challenging him to a gunfight and you'll meet him outside on the street. Then, quickly back out the door while keeping your eyes on him. Go east down Main Street about twenty yards from the front of the saloon."

"That way, you can watch the doors as he comes outside. If he says he doesn't want to fight, call him a coward. If that doesn't work, go outside and move his horse across the street to my shop. If he thinks you're stealing his horse, that'll piss him off," advised Tom.

Cody realized that what Tom and Jeb said made sense and agreed that their plan was a good one. The men followed him out of the stable and up the street to Tom's shop. Jeb and Tom would wait there.

Cody was already getting angry. He'd try and act even angrier once he got inside the saloon. He remembered Tom's warning not to get too angry because it could affect his timing. Cody trotted up the middle of the street to the saloon.

He stood outside for a minute to compose himself for what was about to happen. He took a few deep breaths. You can bet he was scared, but Cody had been practicing for two years for this chance and was not going to miss it.

Cody pushed open the swinging doors as he strode into the saloon. He scanned the area and noticed that his quarry was seated with Rachel on the right side of the room at the table closest to the door. Rachel was facing the door, opposite the gunman who was seated on her right. The man didn't even glance at Cody when he entered.

Rachel observed Cody move his head upward, pointing with his chin toward the back of the saloon while shouting loudly, "Dammit Rachel, you've been stepping out on me again."

"No, I haven't Cody."

"I'll take care of you shortly. Get out of my sight!" He watched Rachel immediately rise to her feet and move away from the table, heading toward safety at the back of the saloon. As the man at the table turned his way, Cody recognized him.

"Hey buddy, you're interrupting my talk with the lady," declared Rick.

"She is no longer any concern of yours. Hey, I recognize you. You were one of the men who murdered my father."

"You're full of sheep dip, kid. I didn't kill anybody."

"Don't you remember? Back about two years ago, you and five other men shot down the sheriff of this town in this very saloon." He could see realization come over Rick's face as he remembered what happened. "I'm calling you out to answer for what you did. I'll meet you on the street. Before I leave, I'd like to know where the other men are."

Rick laughed, "Kid, you are just going to get yourself killed young. You're out of your league taking me on. Why don't you come back in about ten years? Then it might be a fair gunfight. Not that it's gonna to matter in a few minutes, but the others are in Denver."

As Cody walked backward toward the doors, he snarled, "Listen up, you bastard. Either you come out in the next few minutes or I'll steal your horse to sell it for what I can get. I'll then come back in here and kill you on the spot. It's up to you, either in here or out there." Cody moved out of the saloon, keeping Rick in sight. Once outside, he stepped down off the wooden sidewalk in front of the saloon and moved into position for the gunfight.

Cody heard Tom say, "Remember all your training. Watch his hands and shoot him in the middle of his chest."

Once Cody was out of sight, Rick thought to himself, *'I should have gone to Taos first instead of coming back this way. I'll take on this kid and kill him quickly, so I can get back to drinking and talking to the lady.'* Rick stood up and pulled his pistol from its holster to make sure he had all six bullets in the gun. It was already full.

Rick was pretty sure he'd need only one bullet anyway. The kid was just a greenhorn. As Rick moved around the table toward the front door, he called to Rachel in the back, "Don't worry missy, I'll be right back after I take care of this kid."

As he pushed open the swinging doors, Rachel replied, "I wouldn't count on it."

Rick laughed to himself. This was going to be easy as pie. As he exited the saloon, Rick looked both ways and saw the kid in the street to his left. He sighed, stepped off the walkway and headed to the right into the middle of the street to take up his position.

Cody was more than a little nervous. His hands were beginning to sweat and his mouth was dry as he watched Rick saunter from the saloon. He wiped his hands on his pant legs and tried to control his breathing.

Rick saw Cody wipe his hands and smiled. Cody's stomach was churning, but not from hunger. He could feel a cold sweat coming from every pore. His heart rate had increased dramatically, and he'd never felt more alive than he did right now.

Cody was confident that he would win the gunfight, but there was always that nagging worry that perhaps he wasn't fast enough. Cody waited until Rick stopped in the middle of the street. He glanced quickly at Frank and Rachel, peering out from the open saloon doors, then turned his head to sneak a peek at Tom and Jeb in front of the gun shop. They looked a little worried.

He pushed these thoughts from his head and concentrated on the gunman in front of him. Cody couldn't see them, but the Wilsons and some of their patrons were watching from the restaurant windows. Cody moved four feet closer to Rick and stopped. The gunman was now about as far away as the cacti at the practice range. Cody got into a slight crouch, comfortably aware that he had become very accurate at this distance.

"Okay kid, I'll let you draw first as an edge."

"I don't need any favors from scum like you. I asked you out, so you draw first."

Rick couldn't believe the nerve of this kid. 'All right, if he wants to die quicker, it's okay with *me.'* Rick opened his stance just a hair, his hand hovering about five inches from his holster. He noticed that Cody was mimicking his motion.

Cody remembered Tom's advice not to focus on the man's eyes, but to watch his hand movement. Cody stared at Rick's hand. Time seemed to stop, and Cody realized that the slow-motion action of his brain was kicking into gear. He observed Rick begin his draw by slapping his hand toward his holstered gun.

As Rick's hand reached his gun butt, he noticed that the kid was already pulling his pistols from their holsters. He heard two blasts before his revolver even cleared the holster. Rick felt a searing pain in his chest as he was pushed back several few feet by the impact. Bright red blood sprayed from both holes in his chest.

The gunman's mind didn't register that he was already dead. Rick's last thought was, '*damn, that kid was fast.*' Rick's lifeless body fell onto its back, hitting the street and raising a cloud of dust and dirt.

Cody had already cocked his pistols for another round as his first shots struck Rick mid-chest about three inches apart. He saw the gunman's shirtfront pucker as the bullets entered and the crimson blood spurt in a widening conical spray from each hole. He watched Rick immediately topple backward from the impact.

Cody remained in the street still holding his guns leveled toward where Rick had been standing for what seemed to be ten minutes, but in fact was only about five seconds. Cody remained motionless as he heard Tom say that the gunfight was over and saw the gunsmith nodding his head.

Tom was quickly by his side. Looking directly into Cody's eyes, he repeated, "Cody, it's over. You can relax now." Cody finally responded and lowered his arms. He didn't remember putting his guns back into their holsters. He was trembling a little, nature's way of releasing all the stress and tension his fear had placed into his body.

Gently touching his shoulder, Tom asked, "Are you okay Cody?"

Cody had to lick his lips before he responded. He was trying to get his saliva working again. "Yes, I'm okay. That was certainly intense. I guess this is what I have to expect each time I get in a gunfight."

"Yes it is, and it really doesn't get any easier either. Let's go into the saloon and have a drink. I think we both need one."

Cody thought for a second, and replied, "These men took everything from me and now it's time I collect some of it back." Cody approached Rick's body, now staring blankly skyward from film-covered dead eyes and knelt by the gunman's side. Cody took one of his father's spare badges from those he always carried in his right pocket, placed it sideways on Rick's chest and declared, "This is for you dad."

Cody then rummaged through Rick's pockets, coming away with $145. Cody decided that he would keep Rick's horse and rig and sell anything else of value from his belongings. He got back to his feet and followed Tom into the saloon for a drink of whiskey. Jeb was close behind, with Frank and Rachel on his heels. They all stood at the bar and Frank poured drinks for everyone. Cody announced that the drinks were on him or, more specifically, on Rick.

Everyone in the saloon congratulated Cody and patted him on the back, but Cody wasn't ready to celebrate what had just happened. Yes, he was happy to be alive after his first gunfight, but he knew that he had a long way to go before his vengeance was complete, if it ever would be. He might chase these men from here to eternity and never catch them. Hopefully, the Gold Rush would continue for a few more years, so he'd have a chance to search for them. He mused that it might not be long before he left Shiprock for Denver.

Cody's stomach was still doing flip flops and he feared that everything might come back up if he continued pouring booze into it. He left money enough for another round for the people left in the saloon, leaned close to Tom and declared, "I want to get out of here. Someone needs to go get Jose to remove Rick's body from the street. We should also take Rick's horse to Jeb's and go through the bedroll and saddlebags. I want Jeb to determine the quality of the animal so that I can decide whether to keep it or trade it to Jeb for a better one."

"All right, Cody. I understand. Let's get out of here and go down to Jeb's." Jeb joined them as Cody pushed through the well-wishers and out the front doors. Cody grabbed the reins of Rick's horse and led it toward the stable. Jeb and Tom flanked him on either side as they walked.

No one spoke all the way to Jeb's. Cody just looked at the ground as he put one foot in front of the other. He seemed to be on auto-pilot with no emotion showing on his face. Tom and Jeb exchanged occasional glances during the silent journey. They knew what had just happened would occupy Cody's mind for a quite a while.

It's hard to kill another human being and not feel remorse about taking a life, even if that life was a bad one. This incident would stay with Cody for the rest of his life, and he'd need to learn how to accept it and move on.

Once they got inside the stable, Cody led the horse to an empty stall. He untied the bedroll from behind the saddle and removed the saddlebags from the horse's back. Cody then removed Rick's .30-.30 Winchester rifle from its scabbard and handed everything to Tom.

"Jeb, can you give me a clear understanding about the condition of this horse? I may want him for my own. But if he has some problems, maybe you can buy him from me and I can purchase a better horse from you."

"Sure, I'll take care of that a little later. Why don't you and Tom head home for the rest of the day? You can worry about the horse tomorrow."

Tom agreed that this was a good idea. "We'll see you later, Jeb." Cody mechanically carried Rick's saddlebags and bedroll. Tom put his arm gently around Cody's shoulder and led him out of the stable toward the house. Tom thought he might fix something to eat if Cody was hungry.

Once they returned home, Cody put Rick's items on the kitchen table and sat down in one of the chairs. Tom stood next to him and asked, "Are you hungry? I can fix you something."

"I don't think I can eat anything right now. My stomach is still upset." Cody pulled the bedroll toward him and opened it. It contained Rick's duster, a white shirt and dark gray pants. Hopefully, the duster would fit him. If not, all of this could be put up for sale at some point. He rewrapped the blanket around the items.

Next, Cody pulled over the saddlebags. He opened the left flap and pulled out a small cast iron skillet and a waxed paper bundle twisted shut at the top with a string tie. This contained five hard biscuits, sometimes called "corn dodgers," which people carried on long journeys. They stayed good for several weeks if they weren't eaten before they needed to be thrown away. There was also a knife, fork and a small canister of salt. Cody returned everything to the saddlebag and retied the flap.

Cody examined the right side of the saddlebag next. He found a box of .45 bullets for Rick's six-gun and another box of ammo for the .30-.30 Winchester. Cody discovered what had once been a black handkerchief but had now faded to a light gray from use, the sun and trail dust.

There was also a folding knife with what appeared to be elk antler sides and a well-worn, three-inch blade. Next, Cody found a small flask of whiskey which was three quarters empty. The last item was on the very bottom. It was a long, heavy, cylindrical bag tied tightly at the top. "I wonder what's in here?"

"I have a pretty good idea what might be in there, and if it is, you may be rich."

Cody propped the heavy bag straight up on the table, untied the top and looked inside. Tom came over and stood shoulder to shoulder with Cody looking down at gold-colored dust. They looked at each other and smiled. "Wow! I wonder where he got this and how much it might be worth?"

"I don't know where he got it, Cody, but that much gold is worth several thousand dollars."

"Really? You think it could be worth that much money?"

"Yes siree. It certainly could be."

Cody closed and retied the bag, then returned it to the saddlebag. He added the rest of Rick's items except the bullets and closed the flap. Cody put the two boxes of ammo on the table and asked if Tom could swap them for .44 caliber bullets for his guns. Tom readily agreed.

"Why don't you try and lie down for a while and rest, Cody? What you just went through takes a toll on your body, especially your first gunfight."

"You can bet on that. It seemed that my whole body was shaking before I drew on Rick."

"That's the exact same thing that happened to me each time I got into a gunfight. It doesn't matter if it's your first or your thirtieth time. Unless you don't have any feelings at all, which some really evil men seem to lack, it's probably true of everyone else."

"How long does this nervousness last?"

"Well, it's different for everybody. It may only take a few minutes, or it can last days. The question is, do you want to carry on your quest for revenge against the others? Sometimes after a first kill, people change their minds about continuing."

"I'm sure that I must continue after the others. If I stop, I'd be letting down my dad."

"I think you father would be proud of what you did today to avenge his murder. I'm not sure how he'd feel about going after the others. That is something you must decide. It really doesn't matter whether it's right or wrong."

"If I was in your shoes and saw my own father's murder, I wouldn't stop until they were all dead. But that's just me. If you do continue, make sure that you keep your father's murder and any anger from that incident with you. It may just save your life when you need it."

Cody rose from the table, got a glass from the cabinet and filled it with water from one of the buckets. He took a long drink, finished it off and refilled the glass. Cody turned to Tom and said, "I feel tired. I think I'm ready to lay down for a while and rest."

Tom said that was a good idea and he'd see Cody later after he got up. Cody closed his bedroom door and placed the glass of water on the small table next to his bed. He flopped down onto the bed on his left side facing the door and began reviewing everything that happened so far today.

Cody kept coming back to the showdown. He saw his bullets hit Rick with enough impact to push him back as the gunman fell to the ground and remembered all the bloody spray that spewed from his chest. Cody was pleased about his bullet placement. He couldn't think of anything he could have done better.

He shuddered a little from the thought of the whole ordeal. Cody hoped to get some rest and closed his eyes, but his mind was too active and kept replaying the gunfight. He tossed for quite a while but eventually fell into a troubled sleep.

After Cody awoke from his nap, he felt a little better and was ready for a meal. He hadn't eaten anything since breakfast and his stomach was growling. He wasn't sure what time it was, but he supposed it was already late in the afternoon. When Cody rose from his bed and opened the bedroom door, he saw Jeb and Tom talking at the table.

"Hi Jeb."

"Hi yourself. How are you doing?"

"I'm doing okay I guess, though right now I feel pretty hungry."

"Well, that's a good sign."

"I'd like to take you both to dinner at Wilson's if that's okay with you."

Jeb was the first to reply, "Well Cody, I never turn down a free meal, especially a good one."

Tom nodded his head in agreement and added with a chuckle, "All right, let's go then, before Cody withers away."

During their short journey to the restaurant, Jeb advised, "Cody, I checked out your new horse. He's a good mover and is about four years old. I didn't feel anything out of place or see any specific problems except some scars from overuse of spurs. The animal should be a fine mount for you. I'd let him eat well over the next few days to rebuild his strength. After that, he should be good to go."

"Thanks Jeb. What about the man's saddle?"

"It's pretty worn from prolonged use over the years. Some of the straps already show a lot of wear and are liable to break at any time. Personally, I'd buy a new one the first chance you get."

As soon as they entered the restaurant, Emma Wilson hurried over exclaiming, "Cody, are you all right? We were all watching from our windows. Was that one of the men that murdered your father?"

"Yes, it was. I'm all right I guess. I'm sure it will take some time to me to get over it. But, right now, I'm awful hungry. Can we get something to eat?"

Mrs. Wilson showed them to their usual table close to the kitchen door. "We have pork chops today. Barney brought in a hog side for us earlier and my husband chopped it up. I'll put some green beans with it and some gravy for the chops. How does that sound?"

Cody hadn't had pork chops since long before his father died. He replied happily, "That sounds wonderful to me."

"That sounds great to me too!" echoed Jeb. Tom just nodded and smiled.

The other customers were staring at Cody like they did after his father was murdered. There was nothing he could do about it, but it still felt a little uncomfortable. People whispered in undertones at their tables and acted like they were even a little afraid of him.

News about the gunfight had spread quickly around town. It seemed that a new fast gun lived right in Shiprock. The question on everyone's mind was whether Cody was going to turn bad like the man he shot or would become a lawman like his father. The townspeople figured that only time would tell.

Since most quick draw shooters were frequently challenged by outsiders to prove who was fastest, the locals wondered just how long Cody might survive and if trouble would come to Shiprock because of him.

A short while later, Mrs. Wilson came out with three warm plates of food. She had put a good portion of gravy on top of the pork chops for them. Cody thought, 'Wow! This sure looks good.' He thanked Mrs. Wilson and all three men dove right in. No one said much until most of their food was gone.

Once his belly was full, Cody asked, "Jeb, would it be okay if I took the next two weeks off? You can get ahold of me if you really need extra help with something."

"Sure Cody, I don't think that'll be a problem."

"What do you plan to do?" asked Tom.

"I want to devote about ten hours a day to practicing my fast draw. Hopefully this will increase my speed even more."

"Well, that sounds reasonable. I don't have much for you to do around the shop either. I'll have to check if I have enough bullets."

"Most of the time I won't need bullets. I plan to work mainly on repetition of movement and dry-firing."

"You'll have to do this pretty much by yourself Cody. I can come out at lunch time to see how you are doing and bring some bullets, just in case."

"Okay, I'd like that. If you could bring something to eat, that would be great too," Cody smiled. Tom smiled too.

The next morning after Tom prepared a breakfast of eggs and bacon, he and Cody left the house together but went in different directions.

Tom headed to the gun shop while Cody hurried to the stable with two full canteens to borrow a mount for his visit to what he felt was his personal gun range.

Once there, he tethered the horse in the usual spot and got down to business. He drew from both holsters, first with the right hand and then with the left. Cody practiced for about four hours before Tom arrived.

"How are things going?" asked Tom as he dismounted.

"Pretty good. I haven't fired my guns yet. I wanted to wait until you got here to help me sight my shots."

"That's fine. I brought some ham, cheese and mustard sandwiches for lunch. Let's take a break and eat." Tom had even gone by the general store and purchased an orange and a grape soda. Cody chose the grape. Flavored sodas were a favorite treat in Shiprock. They'd only been introduced in 1865, but now were also available in peach, pear, pineapple, strawberry, raspberry, cherry and black raspberry.

After the hearty meal and delicious soda, Cody asked, "Has anything of interest happened in town?"

"No, are you expecting something to happen?"

"No, not just yet Tom. But we both know that once any town has a fast gun, it's like a magnet that pulls in other shooters to try their hand at the new gunny."

"Well Cody, I think it's awful early to start worrying about that already."

"You know how people are Tom. They may have already written to their family in other cities and states about the gunfight. Gossip flows freely and spreads like prairie fire, my dad used to say."

"Yeah, well nothing has happened yet. It probably won't for at least a month or close to it anyway. Why do you ask?"

"I've been doing some hard thinking. I'm probably going to leave after my two weeks are up. I've waited long enough already."

"I had a feeling you might be figuring that way when you asked for two weeks of practice time."

"I was going to talk to you about it later today. I hope you're not mad at me."

"Naw, I'm not mad, although I'll be a little lonely when you leave. I've gotten kinda used to having you around. But life always seems to be changing, doesn't it?"

"Yes, it does, but I should get back to practicing. Now I can use bullets, so that you can help me see where they hit."

Once Cody used up all the bullets, Tom announced that he had to get back to work. Tom said Cody's accuracy and speed were improving and, by the time the two weeks were over, he was pretty sure Cody would be even faster.

Tom thought to himself, 'if Cody had practiced this much at one stretch over the last two years, he might have already become the fastest gun that ever lived. In fact, he's not far from that right now. I'm proud of what Cody has accomplished. He can handle any one opponent in a shootout, but I still worry about the boy facing that whole bunch of desperados at one time. I only hope that won't happen.' Cody returned to dry-firing his pistols for the rest of the day. He returned to the house tired, hungry and thirsty about six that evening.

Tom had been waiting for Cody's arrival before he started dinner. "What do you want for supper?"

"I have a taste for pancakes."

"All right. So, how'd the rest of the day go?"

"It went fine. Hey, Tom. I've been thinking. I'm worried that all the dry-firing I'm doing might break some internal mechanism in my pistols. I'm sure I don't know everything about their parts, and I don't want my guns to fail when I need them most."

"Whoa, slow down a minute Cody. Have you forgotten that I'm a gunsmith? When you finish your two-week training, I'll help you break down your pistols. We'll check their innards for wear and tear and replace any damaged parts. I'll make sure your guns are oiled and in perfect working order before you leave."

"You won't have to do a thing to them until after they're fired. I wouldn't practice any more, however, after your pistols are ready. You want them to be in pristine condition to kill those gunslingers." Cody agreed with Tom's plan.

The two weeks of practice went by too quickly
for Cody. He was sure gonna miss Tom and Jeb
when he went away on what he called his "quest."
At the end of every practice, Cody made sure his
guns were loaded. He knew it wouldn't be too
long before some gunny rode into Shiprock to
challenge him.

Hopefully, he'd be on his way to Denver
before anyone showed up. As it turned out,
the danger Cody expected came from a totally
different direction.

Cody was returning to town from his last day
of practice and was only about a mile and half
from Shiprock when he spotted three riders
ahead blocking his path. He knew immediately
that this was not good, but there was only

one trail to town and he wasn't willing to back down from anyone.

As Cody got closer, he recognized Bill and his brothers. Cody wondered if Bill wanted to retaliate for the fight they had some time ago. He'd hoped that losing would have knocked some sense into the guy, but he was a classic bully and probably wanted to get even. Cody assumed this was going to get serious and would most likely end in gunplay with one or more of the Camp boys. Cody slowed down as he neared the trio.

"May I please go by? Tom is waiting for me back in town."

"Aw, can I please go by? No, you can't 'breed," snarled Bill sarcastically. "We're going to settle this once and for all."

Cody sighed as he responded, "Bill, I didn't think you were this stupid. I figured you'd stop bullying me after our fight. I believe someone else must be pushing you." Cody looked sharply at Bill's brothers, one at a time.

"Nobody pushed me into confronting you again. I don't believe that you killed that man in a fair fight. I heard that he'd been in the saloon all day and was stone cold drunk. I understand you've been practicing, but I've been using a gun for years. I think it's high time you pay for humiliating me in front of my family and the whole town."

"You were the one that started the fight, so what happened is on you, not me. I don't want to kill you or either of your brothers if they try to help you."

"Oh ho, so you think you're good enough to take us all on at once? Your head is so far into the clouds, you must believe your own hype. Well, I'm going to put some holes in your ego."

"Bill, please don't do this. You're going to get hurt or worse. I don't need this on my conscience."

One of Bill's brothers declared, "It sounds like Cody is afraid to face you Bill. Maybe you were right that he was only able to kill that man because the guy was drunk."

"I'm done talking. It's time to pay the piper," Bill sneered with a smile. Cody slowly dismounted, watching the three brothers to make sure they didn't pull anything while he was getting off his horse. Cody decided that, if possible, he'd try to shoot Bill in a shoulder instead of taking his life. If his brothers got involved, he wasn't sure he could do the same for them, but he'd try anyway.

As he dismounted, Bill announced, "Just for your information, I've been practicing too. I haven't just been twiddling my thumbs at home. This is your last day on earth Cody."

Cody was twenty-five feet from Bill and both men were moving slightly to each other's left, so that they wouldn't shoot their horses. Cody could still see Bill's brothers clearly, so he'd notice if they started drawing their weapons. Cody tried to reason with his opponent one more time, "Bill, you can stop this now and we can go our separate ways. This is senseless."

"Stop trying to talk your way out of this. It's not going to work."

"All right, I tried. Bill, you go ahead and draw first." Bill smiled and began his draw. He got his hand on the grip and started pulling his gun from its holster when he saw Cody pointing a pistol at him and heard the shot. Orange-red and yellow flame and gray smoke belched from Cody's gun barrel.

The bullet hit Bill in the upper right shoulder and spun him around, a scarlet fountain spurting from the wound. In response, Bill dropped his gun and covered the wound with his left hand. Bill almost fell but caught himself in time to stagger back to his feet yelling, "Dammit!" Neither Bill nor his brothers could believe what had just happened.

Cody had both his guns out now covering Bill's brothers. "Anyone else want to try? If not, get your brother on his horse and ride in front of me back to town." Shaking their heads, Bill's brothers dismounted and helped Bill into the saddle. Cody retrieved and mounted his horse, watching them all very closely.

Once they got into town, locals on the street gawked and pointed at the four riders. Bill and his brothers were still in front of Cody when Tom approached them from the gun shop. Cody ordered the Camps to stop and they did.

"Well Cody, I see there's been a little disagreement. How's Bill?" Tom asked calmly.

"I think he'll be all right, Tom. His brothers are going to take him down to Doc Charles for help." Cody turned back toward the Camp boys and snarled, "If any of you plan on doing anything about this, the next time I'll kill you all. Do you understand?" The brothers nodded nervously. "I don't think I heard you. Say, 'Yes.'"

They all answered, "Yes."

"In fact, if any of you come after me, I won't only kill each of you, but I'll probably be angry enough to go after your mother and father. Do I make myself clear?"

All three Camp boys repeated, "Yes."

"Good. Now take Bill to the doctor. I don't want to see any of you around here for a while." The three frightened Camp brothers immediately began moving down the street toward the doctor's house.

Tom looked up at Cody and asked, "Wasn't that pretty harsh, especially about their mom and dad?"

Cody shook his head and replied, "I want them to think real hard and long about leaving me alone. You know I wouldn't go after their parents, but maybe they're just too dumb to know it. It's a little added incentive for them to be good."

Tom shook his head and returned to his shop. After he dismounted, Cody followed Tom inside. "All right Cody, tell me what happened."

Cody explained that the Camp boys were waiting for him on the trail and that he tried to get Bill to back down, but he wouldn't have any part of it. "I was concerned that his brothers were also going to draw, but they didn't move an inch once they saw my guns pointing at them. I think they were in shock."

"I'm sure they were. I guess they won't pick on anybody for a long time after this. They won't know who's been practicing. That's one good thing to come out of this gunfight, unless they're as dumb as dirt."

"I wouldn't bet on that, one way or the other," Cody chuckled.

"I wouldn't either," replied Tom laughing.

"I'm pretty hungry Tom. How about I treat for dinner at Wilson's?"

"I won't object to that. I'm hungry too."

Cody and Tom strolled down the street, went into the restaurant, headed for their usual table and waited for Mrs. Wilson. She came out of the kitchen and was surprised to see them sitting there. "Hello, how are my two favorite men? By the way, wasn't that Bill and his brothers that came into town with you? Is Bill hurt?"

"Yes, he is. I shot him in the right shoulder. They were waiting for me on the trail back into town. I tried to talk him out of it three times, but you know Bill. He's stubborn as an ox and wouldn't change his mind."

"Do you think they'll try to ambush you again?"

"I doubt it. I kind of implied that I'd kill their whole family if they tried anything. Hopefully, they aren't that stupid."

"You wouldn't really do that, would you Cody?" gasped Mrs. Wilson, holding her hands together protectively against her chest.

"No, of course not. But they don't know that."

"Oh, you two are terrible," Mrs. Wilson chuckled.

"Me! Not me! I didn't have anything to do with this," exclaimed Tom. Cody and Emma Wilson looked at each other and smiled before he and Tom ate their dinner in companionable silence.

When Cody came out of his room the next morning, he noticed Tom at the table cleaning his guns. "You don't have to do that Tom. I was going to do that after breakfast."

"I'm almost done now, so just sit down. I'll fix our breakfast soon." Cody took a seat and watched Tom finish cleaning and oiling his pistols. Tom handed them to Cody so that he could return them to their holsters.

"Have you decided when you are leaving today?"

"About an hour after we finish breakfast, I think." Cody stood up, returned to his room and pulled the bag of gold dust from Rick's saddlebag. He brought it into the kitchen as Tom cooked eggs and bacon for breakfast.

Tom glanced at Cody and asked, "What are you doing with your money bag?"

"I want to transfer some of this gold into a different container. Do you have anything smaller that could hold some of this without spilling?" Cody didn't want to keep the bag, since he didn't know how Rick acquired it. Someone might recognize it and believe that he had stolen it.

"Let me think on that. I don't have anything here for the gold. I might have something at the shop, but why don't you go over to the dry goods store and see if they have any empty perfume bottles? They'd do the trick."

Okay. I'll check it out and meet you at the shop."

After breakfast, Cody packed a new set of eating utensils and the clothes he was taking into a longer, wider bedroll he'd purchased yesterday from the dry goods store. He put the rest of his belongings into Rick's saddlebags. He'd thrown everything else away except the frying pan, which he'd cleaned thoroughly.

Meanwhile, Tom made some sandwiches for the road and included some bacon and biscuits. Cody thanked him and added the food to his saddlebags. He made sure to fill his two large canteens with water for the trip, too.

Cody looked around the house, trying to fix it in his mind. It might be some time, if ever, that he'd be able to return. Tom headed for the shop while Cody visited the dry goods store. He found two empty perfume bottles, each of which looked like it would hold about half the gold. After Cody paid for them, he went to the gun shop.

Once inside, Cody brought his saddlebags and the two vials into the back room. He pulled out the gold sack and opened both bottles on Tom's work bench.

"Wait a minute Cody. I have something that would work good for pouring the gold." Tom found a funnel on the second shelf down on the left side of his work bench and set it into the first empty bottle. He held it steady as Cody opened the gold bag and started to pour.

The golden flakes fell in a steady stream through the funnel. They resembled sand falling in an hour glass but were much prettier. In twenty-five seconds, the vial was full. Cody stopped pouring and Tom tapped the funnel to shake any remaining dust into the bottle.

Cody put down the bag, placed the cork into the neck and gently tamped it down to ensure a very snug fit. They did the same thing with the second bottle. Once all the gold had been transferred, Cody placed one vial in the bottom of the right saddlebag. He handed the other and the empty gold sack to Tom.

"Cody, what are you doing?"

"I want you to have these for everything you've done for me, in case you need money for any reason. I may not be back for a while or, if fate ordains otherwise, ever," replied Cody smiling.

"I can't accept this! This gold is yours. I tell you what. If you'd like, I'll hold onto this for you until you return. If, and I say if, I need to borrow some of this gold, I'll pay you back later."

"If that makes you feel better, then fine, have it your way."

Tom smiled at Cody's words. He then became serious and declared, "You might want to convert the dust into paper money when you reach Farmington. That way no one can question where you obtained the gold."

"That's a really good idea. I'll do just that."

"Remember to keep looking over your shoulder every few minutes. Always be vigilant for possible violence. My prayers are with you on this quest of yours. Please come back when you can," pleaded Tom. Cody said he would, hugged the gunsmith tightly, picked up his saddlebags and left the shop. Tom followed Cody out to his horse as Cody placed his saddlebags over its rump. As he mounted, Tom called, "Take care son."

"You take care of yourself too. Look in on Jeb occasionally, will you? I'm going to see my parents one last time before I leave. I'll be seeing you." Cody waved before turning his horse and jogging away toward the cemetery.

Leaving his mount at the entrance, Cody walked over to his parents' graves. He had visited them at least twice a month since his father was murdered, usually spending at least half an hour giving them the latest news about everything that was going on in his life.

"Hi mom, hi dad. I'm leaving Shiprock for what may be a long time, so I've come to say goodbye to you both. Mom, I know that young Navaho braves as they come of age have always undertaken a vision quest to seek their future path. Like my ancestors, it is now time for my own quest, but I have already chosen my direction. I intend to seek retribution from each of the men that murdered dad and will not return until I have administered justice to them all. Whether or not you agree with this decision, I must do this for you and for myself. Please have my ancestors look with favor on this journey and provide me their blessings and luck in achieving my quest. I love you both very much and will visit you when I can."

Cody turned from his parents' gravesites and strode purposefully from the cemetery. He mounted his horse and, without a backward glance, sped eastward toward his destiny.

Cody took Tom's words to heart and looked around every few minutes. He didn't want to get caught with his pants down. The journey to Farmington, New Mexico was uneventful. Cody arrived at the outskirts of the city shortly after 4:30 in the afternoon. He'd pushed his pace to Farmington, so that he could make it to the bank before it closed.

Cody looked at all the buildings that had been erected over the years. This place was definitely large. He saw all types of businesses: a general store, the cattleman's company, a realtor, a clothing shop and a gunsmith; as well as several hotels, some restaurants and many saloons.

Cody rode slowly down the street until he spotted the bank. He thought, *'this must be a successful bank. All the hitching rails in front are full.'* Cody stopped, dismounted and tied his horse in front of a saloon just to the right of the bank. Cody would discover the real reason the rails were full only a few seconds later.

He heard shots and a woman's scream from inside the bank just before the front door was flung open and three armed, masked men appeared. One stood on the wooden walkway peering down the street in the opposite direction from where Cody stood.

A second was slowly backing out the door, his gun covering whoever was still inside. The third and closest to Cody, was on the walkway starting to turn toward him. Each man held a bank sack bulging with money in one hand and a gun in the other that swayed back and forth as they looked in all directions.

Cody was startled when the shots rang out and now he carefully watched the outlaws to see what they would do next. The nearest man turned even further in his direction. Since Cody was a son of a sheriff, he knew that the robbers might try to shoot anyone that they saw. He wasn't going to wait to find out. He had somewhere else to be and needed to be alive to do it.

The man was now staring directly at him and was almost in position to fire his gun. Cody quickly drew both his pistols and shot him. He watched in slow-motion as his bullets puckered the man's shirtfront on each side of the heart. Small dust clouds rose up and out from the holes, and blood spurted for several feet in a gruesome crimson display. The man crumpled backward and fell dead on his left side on the walkway in front of the bank, but not before his gun finger spasmed and sent a bullet into the wooden planks.

The man who backed out of the bank then turned toward him. Cody shot him next, since the other robber was still looking in the opposite direction. Cody's bullets hit the man in the right side of his chest. Again, he watched dust and scarlet blood rise upward and spew from the outlaw's body as he collapsed.

The final man now wheeled toward Cody. He spotted both his partners already on the ground and began firing, even before locking his gun on his target. Cody shot the robber three times, striking the man twice in the chest and once in the throat. Once more, ruby red blood and dust flew from the wounds. The man's head jerked sharply backward from the impact of the bullet to his neck. He was the only gunman to fall off the wooden sidewalk into the dusty street. Cody had killed all three bank robbers in under ten seconds.

The people on the street when the robbery took place had scurried to find hiding places when the shooting started. Now that Cody had lowered and holstered his guns, they began to emerge and move toward the bank and the dead gunmen.

The local marshal and a deputy ran the fifty yards from the jail to the bank with their guns drawn, yelling for everyone to stay back until they got the situation under control. They jumped onto the walkway, verified that the robbers were dead and then entered the bank to check on things inside.

Cody stood next to his horse and waited for the lawmen to complete their business. Several minutes passed before they reappeared and began questioning the townspeople. The locals pointed at Cody and advised that he had killed all three gunmen. The marshal stepped off the walkway and approached Cody, who was still nervous from his encounter with the robbers. He asked, "Are you the man who killed the bank robbers?"

Cody swallowed first before responding, "Yes, I am responsible for killing the three bank robbers." The marshal asked his name and what he was doing in Farmington. Cody gave the man his full name and explained that he was just passing through town and had stopped by the bank to exchange some gold for cash. Cody also mentioned that he was the son of the sheriff in Shiprock.

The marshal introduced himself as Ben Parker and declared, "I knew you father, Cody. He was a good man. I hadn't seen him in a year or two before he was killed and I'm very sorry that he died."

"Thanks marshal. It seems that I just happened to be at the wrong place at the right time."

Smiling, the marshal replied, "Well, you certainly did this city a favor by protecting its money and its citizenry from those bank robbers."

"Did anyone inside get hurt? I heard shots."

"Yes, unfortunately a male bank clerk was killed. Evidently, he tried to pull a gun on the robbers. I told the manager to close the bank for the day. You can spend the night free of charge in our best hotel for your quick action and complete your business in the morning, if that's okay with you."

"Yes, that would be fine. It's getting late anyway. I could use a good bed and dinner tonight. Can you direct me to where I need to go?"

"Go to the hotel across the street over there," the marshal pointed. "Tell them that I sent you and want them to give you their best room. I'll come over after I'm finished here to set things straight with their management. Why don't we have dinner together tonight?"

"Thanks again marshal, that sounds good. I guess I'll see you soon."

Cody turned away after the marshal returned to examining the dead gunmen. He unhitched his horse and led it across the street to the front of the hotel. Cody tied it to a pole where the animal could easily reach the horse trough. Cody then took off his bedroll, rifle and saddlebags and carried them into the hotel. He approached the front desk and spoke to the man behind the counter.

"The marshal told me to come here and ask for your best room. He'll be over to speak to you right after he takes care of things at the bank."

As he handed Cody a key, the clerk replied, "We'll take care of you, mister. You can have room three at the front of the hotel. It's our best room."

"Thanks. Does your hotel have a restaurant?"

"Yes, sir. It's one of the best in the city."

"Good. When he arrives, please be so kind as to tell the marshal which room I'm in so that he can visit me."

"I certainly will."

Cody turned to his right and trudged up the stairs to his room. He unlocked the door, carefully relocking it after he was inside. Cody dropped his belongings onto a nearby chair and sank wearily onto the bed. His hands were still trembling from the encounter at the bank. Cody assumed this was leftover tension trying to leave his body. He decided to lay down until the marshal arrived.

A half hour later Cody heard a knock. He stood up, approached the door and asked who was there. After the marshal identified himself, Cody unlocked the door and welcomed Marshal Parker into his room. The marshal asked if the room was satisfactory. Cody laughed and replied, "This is the best room I've ever seen, let alone slept in."

Smiling, the marshal declared, "Good. I'm glad you like it. I thought we could have dinner at 6:30 tonight at the restaurant in this hotel after I get the bodies and personal property of the bank robbers secured."

"As to their property marshal, since I was the one to remove these men from the living, can I have the money in their pockets, their horses and anything of value in their belongings after you take out the cost of their burials?"

The marshal looked at him quizzically and replied, "Well, that's not how we generally work things around here. Are you a bounty hunter?"

"No. I just assumed that the property of anyone I legally kill belongs to me. I'm on my way to Denver and every little bit would help. Do you know if these men were wanted?"

"Not that I know of, but I'll check the wanted posters in my office once I get back there. I'll also do some thinking on your other question and let you know at dinner."

"All right, that's fine by me. I'll see you downstairs about 6:30 then." After the marshal left, Cody removed his gun belt, relocked the door and laid back down. Cody slept for about an hour. When he awoke, he checked his father's watch and found that he had about ten minutes before he was supposed to meet the marshal.

On top of the chest of drawers in front of his bed was a wash basin, a pitcher of water and a hand towel. Cody stood up, poured some water into the basin and splashed some on his face. He cupped his hands to scoop more water onto his face, then toweled off.

Cody didn't fully trust the hotel with his valuables, so he took the bottle of gold from the saddlebags put it in his pocket. He was glad it didn't make too big a bulge. He stuffed all his paper money into his other pocket. Cody put on his gun belt, opened the door, stepped into the hallway and relocked it. He went downstairs and spied the restaurant across the hotel lobby through a doorway. There were several chairs in the lobby, so he decided to take a seat until the marshal appeared.

The marshal arrived a few minutes later. Cody got to his feet when he saw him enter the hotel. Marshal Parker looked in Cody's direction and asked if he was hungry. When Cody nodded, the two entered the restaurant and were shown to a table by a waiter. They both ordered steak, potatoes and green beans.

"I've been thinking about your request. I'd need to run it by the city council, but I doubt that they'd agree to it, you being a stranger to the city and all. I haven't looked at the wanted posters yet, either. I am authorized to pay you the bounty on any of the robbers that were wanted. Once we finish eating, I'll head back to the jail and check the posters."

"I understand. We don't have a town council or an elected mayor in Shiprock. I guess I'll have to abide by your local rules. I'll stop by the jail tomorrow morning after I go to the bank. I can't complain though, since you did treat me to a fine room for the night."

"Yeah. I squared it with the hotel manager earlier today."

"Thanks. Hopefully, one of the bank robbers is on a wanted poster. If not, it's not the end of the world."

After eating dinner and a slice of cherry pie, the marshal declared, "I talked to a lot of people who witnessed your interaction with the gunmen. They said you had a blazing fast draw and it took you only about ten seconds to put them down. Let me ask you Cody, would you consider being a deputy here in Farmington?"

"I appreciate your offer, but I have to meet some people in Denver. Once I'm done there, I'm not sure what I'm going to do. Most likely, I'll head back to Shiprock for a while. If I change my mind, can I get back to you?"

"Sure. My offer is always open. I really appreciate your help today. The robbers took almost $5,000 from the bank and that would have hurt the city. You'll be welcome here any time."

The men paid for dinner, left the hotel and parted ways. Since it was still too early to hit the hay, Cody decided to explore the town. He spent almost an hour strolling down the streets. At least five Shiprocks could fit inside Farmington's total area.

The locals seemed friendly. Most of them nodded and said hello as he passed. Along Main Street near the hotel, some of the people that hid when the gunfire started even approached him and shook Cody's hand to thank him.

All the attention made Cody feel self-conscious, but he graciously returned their thanks anyway. The general store was still open, so Cody went inside and purchased some cherry and grape-flavored hard candy. He'd enjoy these on his trip to Denver. Soon after that, Cody returned to his room and went to bed.

The next morning after a good breakfast of buckwheat pancakes with honey and three pieces of bacon, Cody collected his things from the room and returned his key. He'd already put the bottle of gold into his right pocket because he planned to head over to the bank before going to the jail to speak with the marshal.

Cody walked across the street and entered the bank. Inside, he saw two tellers working behind a counter and separated from customers by metal bars. There was a small gap in the bars in the front of each teller with a little door that the teller could close to completely cover the opening. Cody found this all new and interesting. There were two people ahead of him in front of each teller, so Cody had to wait in line.

As he passed the time looking around at the bank's fine furniture, Cody noticed a man sitting behind a desk separated from the bank lobby by a fence-like structure. The fence had a swinging door which the man could open, presumably for customers. Cody walked to the edge of the fence, and spoke to the man behind the desk, "Excuse me sir. I have some gold I'd like to exchange for paper money. Do I have to wait in line at the tellers or is there someone else who can help me?"

The man glanced up from some paperwork and recognized the young man standing on the other side of the fence. He stood up, came around the desk and opened the swinging door. "Well, well, I'm glad you came into my bank today. I haven't had the chance to thank you for what you did yesterday. I can certainly help you. Please come in. I'm the bank manager, William Shepard."

He shook Cody's hand and invited him to take a seat in one of the chairs in front of his desk. Cody pulled the bottle of gold from his pocket and handed it across the desk to the bank manager.

"Well, you surely have a good amount of gold here. Do you want to exchange a little of it or all of it?"

"I'd prefer to exchange it all. I really don't like to carry it around. It's too much of a temptation for other people if they know I have gold."

"I know how you feel. Let me go fetch our balance scale and weights and I'll get you taken care of."

Mr. Shepard momentarily disappeared into a back room and quickly returned with the items. He opened Cody's bottle and poured all the gold into a little pan on one side of the scale. He then began adding metal weights on the other side until the pans were level. The scale indicated that Cody had thirty-three ounces of gold. In 1885, the value of each ounce was $20.69. Therefore, Cody would receive $682.77, minus two dollars the bank charged for the conversion.

"Why, you are now a rich man. How do you want this broken down?"

Cody took a few seconds to think and replied, "I'd like six hundred-dollar bills, one fifty-dollar bill, two tens and the rest in ones, please. That way I won't have a large bulge in my pocket."

"I guess so. All right, I'll go get your money and be right back," Mr. Shepard declared smiling. Cody thanked the banker and waited until he returned from the tellers' area. After the manager counted the money into his hand, Cody thanked him again and left the bank for his visit with the marshal.

As Cody opened the office door of the jail, he spotted Marshal Parker behind his desk against the back wall. "Hi Cody. Come over here and sit a minute. I was just going through these wanted posters." Cody obediently took a seat. The marshal was only halfway through the posters when he found one that looked like one of the bank robbers. He read the description and handed it to Cody to see what he thought.

"This looks like the guy in the middle that walked backward out of the bank."

Cody handed the poster back to the marshal, who put it to the side. After he finished scanning the rest of the notices, the marshal declared, "I didn't see any posters that looked like the other two men." Marshall Parker read from the poster he'd set to the side, "This guy's name was

Charlie Betts. He was wanted for bank robbery and cattle rustling. It lists a $400 reward for him, dead or alive. I'll have to send this to the State capitol to get approval for payment. It may take a few days."

"I don't have that kind of time. I tell you what. You send the request and get the approval. I can pick up the money when I come back through town."

"That sounds good to me. We'll do it that way." Cody rose from his chair and put out his hand. The marshal stood up, shook Cody's hand and declared, "Have a good trip. The money will be in my safe when you return."

"Thanks for everything marshal. I'll see you soon." Cody waved and headed for the door.

As he left, he heard the marshal say, "Remember Cody, my offer is always open."

Now eager to be on his way, Cody strode back to the hotel, mounted his horse and took the street headed north out of town that the marshal described for him last night. Cody figured it should take about two weeks to reach Denver if he kept up a steady jog interspersed with periods of walking to keep his mount rested. Cody had picked up some sandwiches from the hotel before he left. He'd be good for a few days and would buy more food as he passed through other hamlets and towns.

As the days and miles went by, the topography changed from arid desert country to low hills and then into mountainous terrain. Cody saw many more trees including Rocky Mountain juniper, spruce, and aspen; but mostly pines such as Douglas fir, limber, lodgepole, pinion and ponderosa. Their needles littered the ground and made a nice cushion for Cody's bedroll. He had started drinking coffee with Tom over the last few months but was careful to clear a two-foot circle down to the dirt for every fire he made for cooking, coffee or to keep varmints away at night. To avoid the risk of setting the forest ablaze, Cody carefully covered the remains of his fires with dirt to smother all the embers that were still warm.

Luckily, there were no surprises during the rest of his trip. It took Cody thirteen days to make it to Denver. He came over a low rise and saw a major city spread across the plains in front of him. The sight of a metropolis twenty times larger than Farmington took his breath away. Cody had never seen any place near this big but supposed that Denver's tremendous size was due to the Gold Rush that had started over twenty years earlier. The 1880 Census showed 35,629 people living in or around Denver.

From the overlook, Cody could see smoke rising from countless chimneys all over the city. It looked like the whole place was on fire. Even the air was thinner up here in the mountains. During the trip it had strained Cody's breathing a little until he got used to the mile-high elevation. Cody shook his head and kicked his horse forward to head toward his destiny.

It was close to five o'clock in the late afternoon when Cody reached the southern edge of Denver. As he rode deeper into the city, Cody passed innumerable saloons, churches, hotels, banks, boarding houses, restaurants, dry goods stores, saddleries, bakeries, doctors' and lawyers' offices, gun shops, livery stables and even bordellos. There seemed to be billions of people moving everywhere, either walking, riding horses or in buckboards.

Cody picked what looked like a nice hotel close to the intersection of Nevada and South Eighth streets. He assumed the gunslingers would chose a place on the outskirts of Denver to make a quick getaway if necessary. Of course, they didn't have to pick the south side of town.

Cody kept his eyes peeled for the desperados he sought and checked the face of everyone he passed. So far, no one looked familiar. Cody decided to stay close to the hotel tonight and eat at the restaurant inside, just in case the gunmen were staying there. After dinner, he'd start checking the saloons surrounding his hotel. If he didn't find the gang within a week, he'd move to another part of the city and continue his search.

When he went downstairs for dinner, Cody was surprised by the prices and variety on the menu:

Dinner Entrees

Baked Trout in Cranberry or White Sauce	$1.50
Roast Beef or Stuffed Lamb	$1.00
Pork Chops with Applesauce	$1.25
Beef Stew with Onions	$1.25
Lamb Tenderloin and Green Peas	$1.25

Desserts

Bread Pudding	$0.75
Mince or Apple Pie	$0.75
Peach Brandy Pastry	$2.00
Rum Omelet	$2.00
Jelly Omelet	$1.75

Cody tried the baked trout with apple pie for dessert. He really liked these new menu options and tried most of them while he stayed at the hotel. The problem was if he kept staying and eating at good hotels in Denver, Cody felt he'd soon be bankrupted by the higher costs in the big city.

Cody sat on the hotel's front porch a good portion of each day to watch the passersby. He decided that this is what he would do for the first two days at each location. After that, he'd walk at least five blocks in every direction from the hotel to continue the search and familiarize himself with the area. The first week, Cody saw no one resembling the gunmen. He decided to search the east side of town next.

Cody waited until early afternoon before checking out so that he could watch more foot traffic. Before he left, he asked the desk clerk for the name of a good hotel on the east side. It took Cody about fifteen minutes to thread through the heavy foot and buckboard traffic to reach his new hotel at the corner of St. James and North Jefferson streets.

Once he'd settled in, Cody repeated his procedure of sitting on the front porch and watching the people passing the hotel. Unfortunately, Cody's hopes were dashed again when, after another week, he hadn't seen anyone remotely resembling the men he remembered.

He moved to Huntington Avenue and Browne Street on the west side, and then to 34th Avenue and Humbolt Street on the north side without spotting any of the men he sought. Cody began to fear that perhaps they'd already left Denver, but he decided to try one more time in the exact middle of the city.

Cody transferred to a nice mid-city hotel at Fifth and Saguache streets. *'I'm really getting spoiled living like this. I figure I've put on a few extra pounds, but I'll try and enjoy this life while it lasts.'* When he still hadn't seen anyone familiar after four days, Cody wondered if he'd ever find any of the gang in the tide of humanity within the city.

Lucky for him, late in the afternoon of the fifth day, Cody thought he spied someone that looked like one of the gunmen. The man was strolling northward up Fifth Street toward the center of the city. Cody leaped from his seat and followed the man for two blocks until the fellow entered a saloon at the corner of Fifth and Carbon streets. Cody wanted a closer look to make sure, so he followed the guy into the saloon.

The interior was darker than the sunlit street and it took a minute for Cody's eyes to adjust. He took up a position at the end of the bar nearest the doorway, glancing around to locate the man.

When a bartender approached, Cody ordered a beer.

He didn't want to have anything more potent that might impair his faculties and planned to nurse this drink for as long as necessary. He spotted the fellow at a table in the back of the saloon. The guy had joined four other men Cody didn't recognize in a game of poker.

Cody had never played much poker with his father, but Tom had begun to teach him the basics as a way to pass the time if no book was handy. Although he knew the rudiments of the game, Cody didn't want to expose himself by playing poker with his quarry. He just wanted to watch the players to see if any of the other killers might appear.

Eventually, Cody decided to move closer to get a better look at the fellow. He ordered another beer and took it to an open table two away from the poker players. Cody chose a seat that directly faced the man. At this distance, Cody could clearly see the guy's face and recognized him as the gunman that his dad had shot in the shoulder.

Elated to have finally found another member of the gang that killed his father, Cody deliberately kept his gaze averted so his interest would not alarm his quarry. Two hours later, the game was still going strong.

Cody decided to leave the saloon and find a nearby vantage point to continue observing everyone who arrived and departed. Cody hoped that the rest of the gang would join their poker-playing comrade or that this man would lead him to their lair. Cody got to his feet, glanced one last time at the man called Jorge and casually strolled outside.

Cody took a seat on a chair in front of a general store almost directly across the street with an unimpeded view of the saloon entrance. He sat for another few hours before Jorge wobbled back onto the street. His unsteady gait indicated that the gunman had downed quite a few drinks while playing poker. Cody got to his feet and followed him northward on Fifth, taking care to remain far enough behind to remain undiscovered.

Jorge turned left down Pearl Street and was momentarily out of sight. By the time Cody rounded the corner, the fellow was nowhere to be seen. 'Where in the hell did he go?' Cody checked all the establishments on both sides of the street but didn't spot Jorge.

'He must have walked more quickly than I thought and turned again at the next corner.' Cody hurried to the intersection and scanned in both directions, but the gunman had disappeared. Cody swore in frustration and headed back toward his hotel. *'Since this guy visited that saloon once, he'll most likely return there again in the next few days.'*

Cody was hungry and stopped on the way to order bar-b-que spare ribs at one of the local restaurants. He had seen another man eating them yesterday and was anxious to try them for himself. Although bar-b-que sauce was created in the seventeenth century in the eastern U.S. colonies, it was unknown in Shiprock. The ribs were delicious and, of course, Cody ordered apple pie for dessert.

After dinner, Cody returned to his hotel and settled into a chair on the balcony to keep looking for the gunmen. Although he didn't recognize anyone, he had now located a place that one of them had already visited.

He planned to return to the saloon tomorrow afternoon and each day after that until Jorge reappeared. Every morning, Cody walked five or six streets in each direction from the saloon, carefully noting their names and the businesses he passed. That way, the next time he followed the gunslinger, he would be familiar with the area.

Three days later, Cody was sitting across the street from the saloon that this fellow evidently liked to frequent when he spotted Jorge a second time. Cody was surprised, however, that today the gunslinger approached from the opposite direction than before.

Cody again followed the gunman into the saloon, but this time chose a position at the far end of the counter with a good view of the poker table. Unfortunately, Cody didn't recognize any of the other players. He ordered a beer and waited at the bar, glancing over occasionally to observe what was happening at the table and check to see if any of the other gang members arrived.

After he finished his beer, Cody went back outside and crossed the street. He walked a few doors further north on Fifth and found a seat in front of another hotel. Jorge had arrived from this direction and Cody hoped he'd leave the same way. He still had a clear view of the saloon, and this observation point was even closer to the Pearl Street intersection where Jorge had turned left and disappeared before. Cody waited two hours before the gunslinger exited the saloon, ambled past him and again headed west on Pearl. Cody leaped to his feet, ran to the corner and trailed behind Jorge, following more closely this time.

Three blocks later, Jorge turned right and continued north on Oak Street until he entered a two-story saloon near the Agate Street intersection. This was the first multi-floor saloon Cody had ever seen. He peered inside over the swinging entry doors and noticed Jorge at the far end of the bar. Cody glanced up toward the second floor and realized that it was designed to shield customers that wanted more privacy from public view.

Cody entered the saloon and took a seat at a table across the room from the bar. He ordered a beer when the barkeep came over, kept an eye on Jorge and scanned the room for the other killers. Hopefully, this man was waiting for his partners to arrive. As he nursed his drink, Cody noticed that Jorge occasionally glanced his way. Cody felt a twinge of nerves as the gunslinger moved away from the bar and stopped on the other side of his table.

"Hey, I've seen you before. You were just at the other saloon and I believe you've been following me."

Cody stood up and declared, "You're right. I have been following you. I was hoping that you'd lead me to your other friends."

"I don't like anyone following me," the gunman snarled menacingly. "Why are you after me kid?"

Unbeknown to Cody, at that very moment Jorge's three partners were sitting at a private table above him on the saloon's second floor. Jorge's raised voice drew Jim's attention, and he began listening and watching the scene below from behind a curtain. He didn't like the situation at all and immediately alerted the others at their table. Jim feared Cody might be a policeman and the gang was now under suspicion for their robberies. If he wasn't a lawman, they'd have to get rid of this young kid. They didn't want anyone snooping into their affairs.

"You don't remember me, do you?"

"No, I don't kid. Why should I remember you?"

"I was the kid crying over my father's body on the floor of the Shiprock saloon after you and your friends murdered him. Remember? He was the sheriff that shot you in the right shoulder. I hope it still hurts like hell."

"Yeah, now I remember you and your lawdog father. What do you want from me kid?"

"For you to die, you louse. We can either do it in here or out in the street. It's your choice."

"Why you little asshole! You wouldn't last a second against me kid." Cody quickly strode around the table, stood in front of Jorge and jabbed the gunman's right shoulder sharply with the stiff pointing fingers of his left hand. Jorge jumped back a few feet exclaiming, "Dammit kid, that still hurts!" By now, everyone in the saloon was watching them.

"I'm glad, you bastard. I'll be out in the street, so don't take too long or I'm coming back inside to find you." Cody backed slowly toward the doors while carefully watching the fuming gunman.

"I'll be right out kid. It's your lucky day because it's going to be your last."

"Just make sure I meet you outside, asshole," Cody shouted as he backed through the doors and into the street.

Jorge looked up and saw his partners staring down at him from the second floor. "Can you believe this kid?"

"Just go out there and take care of business. We don't want him trailing us anymore," replied Jim.

"Killing that brat will be my pleasure! I'll be right back, guys." The others left their private table and headed down the corridor to a window at the front of the saloon by the second-floor stairway. They made sure to stay far enough back not to be visible from outside.

Jorge exited the saloon and moved to his right onto Oak Street. Most of the saloon patrons and passersby were now watching the action from a safe distance. The crowd had cleared a wide path behind each of the men in the street. "Too bad you'll have a short life kid. You should have stayed home," Jorge laughed.

"Please tell Rick hello in hell when you get there. I killed him two months ago in Shiprock."

"You bastard! Rick was a friend of mine. I admit you've got grit, but Rick wasn't as fast as me. He was probably drunk, too."

"I'll let you draw first old timer, since I can see you're a little nervous."

Jorge grinned and laughed maliciously as he began his draw. Cody's mouth was dry and he felt a few nerves stirring, but nothing like his first two gunfights. He guessed that he was getting callused about these events. As always, everything seemed to happen in slow motion. Cody stared at Jorge's right hand as it moved toward his holster. He waited for the gunny to grab the grip and begin his draw. Cody's pistols were out and leveled before Jorge's gun even cleared the holster.

Cody's bullets hit Jorge mid-chest about an inch apart, as smoke and yellowish-red flame belched from his guns. A crimson fountain gushed like an open fire hydrant from the gunslinger's heart into the street. Jorge died instantly. The impact threw him back several feet and his arms flew into the air as he toppled over on his back, still clutching his revolver. He hit the earth hard.

The dust hadn't yet settled from Jorge's impact when Cody stood over him. Cody quickly holstered his guns, removed a silver sheriff's badge from his right pants pocket, knelt and placed it sideways on Jorge's chest. "That's another one for you dad," he whispered.

As they prepared for their gunfight, neither Cody nor Jorge were aware that the captain of the Denver police was striding down Oak Street in their direction. He was within ten yards of Cody when he announced, "Don't move, I'm the police."

Cody looked up from the dead gunslinger to face a drawn revolver pointed directly at his head by a man hurrying toward him. Cody slowly got to his feet, making sure not to make any quick moves. As the man stopped a few feet away and looked down at the corpse on the ground, he saw that Cody had placed a badge sideways on the body.

"We discourage the practice of gunfighting within city limits. Why did you place a lawman's badge on this man?"

"My father was the sheriff of Shiprock, New Mexico. He was murdered by this guy and five other men. I made a promise at my dad's grave that I would hunt down his killers and exact revenge. I place a badge on their bodies as a final gesture in his honor. Hopefully, it will frighten the three remaining murderers." Some of the locals shouted to the captain that the young man did not draw first and that he shot in self-defense.

Inside the saloon, Big Bob, Jim and Alfredo had watched the gunfight and couldn't believe that Jorge had lost. They had witnessed first-hand the kid's incredible speed. This scared the crap out of each of them.

"None of us are anywhere near as fast as this kid. He's making me very nervous. What are we going to do?" asked Alfredo.

"He doesn't know yet that we're still in Denver. Right now, we should leave here by the back door so that the kid doesn't see us, return to our boarding house and plan our next move," replied Big Bob. Looking around nervously, the gang quickly made their escape.

In front of the saloon, the police captain took a closer look at the body and declared, "Hey, I know this guy. He worked as a guard at one of the local mines and helped escort their gold to the bank. I supervised the deputies at that bank that guarded the shipments."

"Well, if he was a guard, maybe the others are too, either at the same place or another local mine."

"That could be a possibility, since gunnies are often hired as guards," replied the captain, finally holstering his weapon. "Regardless, as captain of the Denver police, I have sworn to protect these citizens and I don't want any more gunfights in my city. Do I make myself clear?"

"Yes sir. I won't start anything, but if one of the other men I'm hunting comes after me I have the right to protect myself."

"Fair enough. Just don't spend too long in Denver. I watched you in action from a long way off and I've never seen anyone that fast. Things tend to get crazy and definitely don't change for the better when a fast gunny is in town."

"Okay captain, I'll only stay around long enough to determine if the other men are also living close to the middle of Denver or are guards at the mines. Hopefully, it won't take me long to find out."

As more of the captain's men arrived on the scene, Cody asked, "Is it okay with you if I take any money in this guy's pockets? I feel that the assets of the men I kill belong to me. This fellow had a horse when he left for Denver and his gun and belt are also worth money. Therefore, unless there's some Denver ordinance stating that all property of the deceased belongs to the city for the cost of his burial, I'd like to have it."

"That seems unreasonable son, but I can't blame you for trying. In most larger towns and cities, unless a dead gunman has family around, all his belongings go toward the welfare of the city and to pay for his burial."

"In that case, can we check at your office to see if he was wanted? At least I can claim the reward for him if there is one." As he spoke, Cody scanned the crowd to see if any of the onlookers were other gang members, but he didn't spot any familiar faces.

"Just let me talk to my men for a minute and then we can head back to police headquarters. It's only three blocks away, close to the geographic center of the city. By the way, my name is Edward Harris."

Cody put the name into his memory. He might need this information in the future. Cody accompanied Captain Harris to police headquarters and climbed the stairs to his office on the second floor.

"We have a clipboard with the latest wanted posters. I'll get one of my men to bring it to you. You can use the table next to the door to search through the notices."

"That would be great."

The captain yelled for the wanted posters, and an officer carried the clipboard to his desk in only twenty seconds. He handed it to Cody who quickly sat down and began searching through the pages. The newest posters were on the top of a thick pile, going back for the past five years. Cody was surprised that there were so many wanted men. He had gone through over three quarters of the stack and began to wonder if any of the gunman were there.

Finally, Cody spotted two faces on one poster that he recognized, Alfredo Torrez and Rick Brenner. Brenner was the man he had killed in Shiprock. The pair were wanted for rustling and the possible murder of cattle owners that later lost stock. The poster offered a $300 reward for each man.

Cody brought the poster to Captain Harris. "You can stop looking for Rick Brenner. I killed him almost three months ago. I'm still searching for his partner, Alfredo Torrez, along with two other gunmen." Unfortunately for Cody, Jorge Rangel wasn't wanted, so he couldn't collect any reward.

"Well captain, it looks like Jorge wasn't a wanted man, so I guess I can't collect anything." Cody told the captain about his encounter with the three bank robbers in Farmington. He wasn't allowed to obtain their valuables either, but since one of the men was wanted, the marshal sent to the capitol for the reward and Cody planned to pick up the money when he came back through town.

After hearing Cody's complete story, the captain declared, "I'll make you the same deal that the marshal made in Farmington. I'd like you to work on the Denver police force. What do you say?"

"Thanks, captain, but as I told the marshal, I need to find the last three men who murdered my father before I can make any other plans."

The Captain said he understood and would also keep a job open for Cody. Cody said farewell and stode back to his hotel, watching every face as he walked down each street.

The three surviving gang members rapidly reached their boarding house at Walnut and Granite streets, two blocks north and two blocks west of the saloon. They had something very important to discuss and, although no other saloon in this part of town had the special amenity of hidden tables on the second floor, these could never be as private as individual rooms with walls. They went to Big Bob's room for a powwow about what to do next. Once safely inside the room, both Jim and Alfredo voiced their concerns about this new problem.

As usual, Big Bob began the discussion. "Dammit, guys, we aren't done stealing from the other mines yet."

"It's true that we've pulled three jobs already with no problems so far, but now with Jorge gone and this kid following us, it changes things," replied Jim. He continued, "I don't mind taking chances for gold, but I don't want to continue with that kid hanging over our heads. He might find out who we are and hit us in the middle of a job."

"Besides, we have enough gold right now that we'll never have to work again. I say we split the gold and leave Denver before the kid or the local law figures out what we've been doing and finds us," added Alfredo.

"I'd hate to let all our plans go to waste. I'd like to finish what we started and hit the other two mine shipments, but I must agree that we might have to stop because of this kid," responded Big Bob.

Jim and Alfredo were talking back and forth about whether to finish the gold heists or to cut and run with what they had already stolen. During their conversation, Big Bob was silently weighing the options. Maybe they could get rid of the kid first and then resume the robberies. They could ambush him the same way they killed the other guards. Of course, this would require some more thought and planning. Alfredo's idea to cut and run also had merit, especially since the gang was now short two men, Jorge and Rick.

Big Bob decided that all of them should vote on the two options and summarized the choices: "Do we split the take and run, or kill the kid and then hit the last two mines? I'm greedy by nature and I vote to stick with our original plan, but we'll need to kill the kid first."

"I vote to cut and run. There's a good change that one or all of us could die if we confront the kid," said Alfredo.

"I kind of like both options. I'm greedy like Bob, but I'm not afraid to say that this kid scares the hell out of me. We'd have to come up with a good plan to get rid of him. Of course, we'd also have to find at least one more guy to help in the robberies. I guess we could get rid of him once we've completed all the heists," said Jim.

"All right, why don't we try and ambush the kid at night like the others? If that doesn't work, then we can cut and run," declared Big Bob. Jim and Alfredo weren't thrilled with the idea, but they agreed to try this option first and put their heads together to formulate a plan.

The three killers decided that Big Bob would show himself to the kid and lead Cody to a more deserted area where the other two would shoot him from a dark alleyway. The chosen ambush site would need a back exit, so the shooters could make a clean getaway on a different street.

They scouted the area and found a perfect alley just two blocks from the saloon off Jasper Street with a back exit onto Pearl. Now all they had to do to proceed with the plan was locate the kid. Once one of gang spotted Cody, he could quickly relay the kid's location to the others. Then Jim and Alfredo could take their positions in the alley while Big Bob lured Cody into the ambush.

Meanwhile, Cody continued searching the streets for his quarry every morning and checking local drinking spots for the gunmen in a two-block radius around Jorge's favorite saloon in the afternoons and evenings. Two days later, Cody was still visiting saloons at almost eight o'clock at night with no luck finding a familiar face. Cody had already checked eight locations, walking through the larger places and looking over the front swinging doors at the smaller establishments.

Cody was headed into a large saloon on Ash Street near Pearl, just a block south and one block west of where he'd killed Jorge, when Alfredo noticed him and rushed to alert his partners. He met them at the next corner and the gang hurried back to where Alfredo had last seen the kid.

The location was a stroke of luck, as it was only a block from the ambush alley. Big Bob ordered the others to get into position and make sure that he had walked past their hiding place before they fired at Cody. He didn't want Jim or Alfredo accidently shooting him, too.

Big Bob stayed in the shadows on Pearl as he waited for Cody to leave the saloon, peeking around the corner onto Ash. Like most of Denver's main streets, Pearl and Ash were fairly well-lit by candle lamps on poles, usually three on a block. There should be enough light for Cody to identify him at this distance, especially if he raised his eyebrows and opened his eyes wide as Cody looked at him.

Big Bob's plan was to stroll a few feet down Ash until Cody reacted, then walk quickly back around the corner onto Pearl and lead the kid to the nearby ambush site.

When Cody left the saloon, he watched a tall man amble around the corner. A street lamp illuminated his startled reaction and Cody recognized him as one of the killers. Cody didn't run after the fellow because the gunslinger could unexpectedly pop out from behind a building and take a shot at him. Instead, he trotted rapidly behind the guy, just as he did when he trailed Jorge.

As soon as Big Bob turned onto Pearl, he quickened his stride, but made sure he stayed in his pursuer's line of sight. The gunman then made a left at the next intersection. Cody sped up too, trying not to lose sight of his quarry. Cody kept pace as Big Bob cut across the street and took a right at the next corner onto Jasper Street.

As Cody turned onto Jasper, he noticed uneasily that there was more shadow and less light on this street. He felt that something might be wrong with following the gunman in this direction, but he just couldn't put his finger on it. Cody had learned young to trust his gut feeling, that little voice or guardian angel that sometimes signals danger.

That inner warning grew louder with every step he took. Nerves tingling and every sense on high alert, Cody moved cautiously ahead on the left side of the street, following the gunslinger while peering carefully in all directions. He spotted a small side alley on the right which was completely shrouded in darkness.

As he neared the opening, Cody heard something thump against wood and then the click of triggers cocking. He whipped out his pistols and covered the alley, twisting and falling sideways toward the ground to make a more difficult target for any gunman. Two shots rang out in quick succession from within the alley, one hitting Cody on the outside of his left arm and the other passing through his right side. He did a sideways tumbling summersault and came up to a kneeling position. Cody returned fire immediately, aiming at the light from the muzzle blasts.

Jim and Alfredo were astonished that the kid had any clue that they were waiting in the alley. As Cody continued firing at the areas where he saw the muzzle flashes, he heard a grunt and then feet running away from the spot. His attention then switched to the next corner where the tall man had disappeared.

When Big Bob peeped around that corner to see if his partners had killed the kid liked they'd planned, he was very surprised that he had to duck for cover when a bullet took out a chunk of wood just above his head, quickly followed by another shot in his direction.

'*There's no way I'm sticking around with this kid after me!*' Big Bob sprinted down the street, tore around the next corner, and kept zig-zagging north and west for blocks. Only after he made sure Cody wasn't following him anymore, did the winded gunslinger double back east toward the boarding house.

Meanwhile, Jim and Alfredo scurried down the alley and turned west down Pearl. Jim walked rapidly, and Alfredo limped behind him with a through and through along his right thigh. It bled, but Alfredo held his hand against the river of red to staunch the bleeding the best he could.

Not many people were out, so the pair didn't attract much attention. With Alfredo groaning slightly as he struggled to keep pace with Jim, they kept moving until they made a right and headed north on Willow Street, both looking back every ten seconds to make sure Cody was not following them.

After sending bullets toward the man at the corner, Cody slowly got to his feet. He holstered his guns and headed back up Jasper Street. Cody was not going to follow the gang members with the wounds he sustained in the gun battle. Although he kept his right hand against his stomach to help control the bleeding, within a few steps Cody's shirt had turned a gory crimson.

Cody staggered back to Ash before running into a policeman who was headed toward the spot where he thought he'd heard gunfire. Realizing that Cody was severely injured, the officer hurried to his side and helped support him as Cody began going into shock from loss of blood. He explained weakly that he'd been ambushed on Jasper and needed to find a doctor.

The policeman helped him stumble a half block to a physician who lived upstairs from his office and eased Cody to a sitting position on the walkway. The officer then pounded on the office door. When no one responded, he ran upstairs and knocked on the door to the doctor's living quarters.

Fortunately, the doctor was home and hurriedly followed the policeman downstairs after the officer explained that a badly injured man needed his help. The two men hoisted Cody to his feet and the policeman helped hold him steady while the doctor unlocked the office door. With Cody between them, they managed to drag him to the first examining room on the right and laid him on a table. Cody was still conscious, but light-headed and dizzy. He hoped he wasn't dying since he still had work to do.

The doctor quickly examined the shallow wound on Cody's left arm and determined that it wasn't serious. He had to cut off Cody's shirt to look at his right side. Once the shirt was removed, the doctor saw an entry wound an inch below Cody's ribcage and two inches toward his middle. He asked the policeman to help turn Cody onto his left side to see if the bullet had exited out his back and was relieved that it had.

He advised the officer that Cody was extremely lucky because the bullet had somehow missed all his major organs. He had lost some blood of course, but it wouldn't be life threatening unless the wound became infected. By this time, Cody had passed out from shock. It took the doctor two hours to clean and stitch both wounds.

The policeman left the office after the doctor began working on Cody, walked into the street and blew the whistle issued to each officer to summon help. After a minute, two other policemen arrived. The man who found Cody repeated what he had been told about a supposed ambush on Jasper Street, not far from their current position, and asked the others to check the area to see if anyone else was hurt or dead.

When they returned, the officers advised that they had found no one and left to resume their scheduled rounds. The first policeman remained at the doctor's office to obtain a more complete report of what had occurred after Cody was awake and alert.

Jim and Alfredo were approaching the boarding house when Alfredo asked, "I'm bleeding like a stuck pig. How far are we from the nearest doctor's office?"

"Quit yer bellyachin' Alfredo. There's a sawbones a block from the boarding house. I'll drop you off there and give the doc a story, but I've gotta get to the boarding house and see if Big Bob made it back." When they arrived, Jim told the doctor that they'd been ambushed in a dark alley and his friend had been wounded. As he left, Jim added, "Alfredo, I'll check to see how you're doing a little later."

When he reached the boarding house, Jim went straight to Big Bob's room and knocked on the door. When the door opened, Big Bob asked, "What the hell went wrong and where's Alfredo?"

After he entered the room and Big Bob locked the door, Jim turned toward him and advised, "Alfredo got shot in the thigh and is at the doctor's office a block from here. I don't know what happened. It seemed like the kid already knew where we were and moved or tumbled to the ground while shooting at us. I think we hit him, but he kept firing. Who or what is this kid? I think we should get out of Denver before he finds us again. We can't spend our gold if we're dead."

"I agree with you, Jim. We need to put a lot of miles between us and that kid. He nearly shot my head off! In the morning, we'll go by the doctor's office and tell Alfredo we're heading out of town. Alfredo had better be able to ride, or we'll leave him here and he can follow us later."

Big Bob and Jim met with Alfredo at the doctor's office and told him what they were going to do. Because he didn't want the others to take all the gold and leave him high and dry, Alfredo assured his partners that he felt well enough to go with them, although he was limping on a crutch given to him by the doctor and his leg really hurt.

The trio paid their bill at the boarding house, saddled up and headed north out of town to their gold cache. They decided to go just over six hundred miles to Kansas City, Missouri, and hopefully live the good life. They were pretty sure the kid wouldn't find them so far away.

They had purchased three more saddlebags and another horse to help carry the gold. It took them only thirty minutes to dig up close to a hundred thousand dollars-worth of stolen gold and transfer it to their saddlebags.

A few days out of Denver, Alfredo was riding ahead as the gang headed east on the main trail. There was nothing in sight in any direction but the endless, empty plains. Big Bob leaned toward Jim and whispered, "I've been thinking over the past two days. Why should we split the gold three ways when we can have it all to ourselves?"

"You know, that makes a lot of sense to me. We could go into business together and make even more money."

"Yeah Jim, that idea is sounding better every minute."

Turning to look at his partners, Alfredo asked, "What are you two gabbing about back there?"

"Well, Alfredo, we're just discussin' how to spend all that gold," Jim replied.

"Me, too, amigos," Alfredo chuckled, turning to the trail ahead.

After Jim and Big Bob scanned the whole vista to make sure no one was nearby, they pulled their guns and shot Alfredo twice in the back. A scarlet spray spurted from his wounds as Alfredo slumped forward on his horse and fell to the ground. He was dead even before he fell.

After Jim caught Alfredo's spooked horse, he and Big Bob took the money from Alfredo's pockets and left him where he fell. They then transferred one saddlebag from the spare horse to Alfredo's mount to share the load. After they remounted, Big Bob looked down at the body and chuckled, "Thanks for all your help, Alfredo. Sorry, but we don't like to share."

Jim agreed, laughing, "That's right partner. Let's get out of here before someone comes along."

The pair spurred their horses to the east as each man pulled a spare pack animal behind his mount.

The next morning, Cody awoke on the examining table. At first, he was confused. His upper left arm ached and a terrible pain in his side wouldn't let him get to his feet. Suddenly, Cody remembered what had happened on Jasper Street. He glanced around the room and saw no one. He croaked out, "Hello" from his parched throat and a man entered the room within a few seconds.

"Well, young man, how are you feeling this morning?" asked the doctor.

Cody swallowed and replied, "Like a mule kicked me in my side. Can I have some water please?"

Chuckling, the doctor replied, "I bet it does, and your side will continue hurting for a while. You were lucky that the bullet didn't hit any of your vital organs as it passed through you. I'll get you a glass of water in a minute."

"I don't feel that lucky right now."

"We can move you to another room in the back of my house where you can stay for a few days."

"Thanks doc, but I don't want to cause you any additional trouble. If you can move me to my hotel, I can recover there."

"We can't move you around too much just yet. I need to keep an eye on you for a few more days to make sure you don't bleed to death. By the way, my name is Doctor Taylor."

When Cody introduced himself, Doc Taylor advised that he already knew Cody's name and added that someone was waiting to see him. The doctor then turned and left the room. A minute later, in strode Captain Harris. 'Oh great!' thought Cody.

"You just can't seem to stay out of trouble, can you?"

"I guess not captain. It seems trouble follows me wherever I go."

The captain smiled and replied, "It seems you're pretty lucky too, or you'd be dead. Tell me what happened."

Cody explained that he was leaving a saloon on Ash when he saw the leader of the bunch that killed his father and tried to follow him back to the rest of his men. "But they must have known I was in town and tried to kill me by ambushing me in that dark alley off Jasper."

"If they tried once, they may try it again and soon. They may already know where you're staying and will ambush you near there when you show up next. My thought is that you move to another hotel to recover. Doc Taylor says you may be laid up for a good two or three weeks."

"I can't wait that long. I need to track them down again before they leave the city."

"Look Cody, you're not in any shape to do anything for a while. If you can give me a good description of the fellow you saw, maybe my men can help you locate these guys. With your information, we can also contact each mine to see if he works at any of them."

"It would be a big help if you'd do that for me, captain."

"I'm not doing this just for you. If these are really bad guys, that gets me to thinking. We've had a rash of gold shipment robberies lately, as well as murders of some guards that worked at different mines. I wonder if these are all connected to your situation? It sure is something I am going to check on, now that I think on it."

"I guess that makes sense. I wouldn't put anything past these guys."

"Get some rest Cody. I'll see you again in a few days." Later that afternoon, some men helped the doctor move Cody to a back room in his house. Cody gritted his teeth to stifle the pain. '*I thought I was tough, but boy, did that hurt!*'

The next day the same men moved Cody to a very good hotel just a few blocks from the doctor's office. It even had room service from the restaurant downstairs. Of course, Cody's wound hurt as he was moved.

The doctor advised that after another five days of bed rest, Cody should start to stand up and try to move around a little because the sooner he started walking, the sooner he'd heal. Cody wasn't worried about the cost of his stay in

Denver, since he still had well over four hundred dollars left in his stash.

If it was possible, Cody hoped that Captain Harris could have the marshal in Farmington wire his money to Denver. As he recuperated in bed, Cody got tired of staring at four walls all day. To stay busy, he asked to borrow some books that the hotel loaned to its customers.

He was still pretty sore after two days and wondered how soon he'd begin to feel normal. Cody was also worried about what the three killers were doing while he was laid up. He was afraid that they might leave Denver. Once they were gone, it would be that much tougher for him to find them again. But right now, he had to concentrate on getting back on his feet. At least the food was good. Cody was eating well but he hated using a bed pan to go the bathroom.

Two days later, Captain Harris visited and asked, "How are you doing, Cody?"

"I'm feeling a little better, but I'm still sore. Have you and your men found out anything more about the men who shot me?"

"No, nothing yet. I sent some of my officers to the mines in the area this morning to see if anyone had quit or not shown up in the last few days. Hopefully, we'll have more information tonight."

Cody thanked the captain for all his help and asked about getting his bounty money transferred from Farmington to Denver.

"Yes, that can be done. First, the marshal will have to get the funds to the bank in Farmington. Then, that bank can transfer the funds to a bank in Denver to pay you here."

"That's good. How can I start the procedure for a transfer?"

"I'll have a bank manager stop by your room with the necessary paperwork, probably tomorrow. I have other things that are a priority right now, so I'll see you soon."

"I can't thank you enough captain."

The captain laughed and replied, "You can thank me best by getting better soon and leaving my city."

"Yeah, I can understand that," Cody chuckled.

The next afternoon, a local bank manager came by his room with funds transfer papers for Cody to sign. He explained the transfer might take up to a week and someone would let Cody know when the money was available in Denver. Cody thanked the man and he left.

That evening after dinner, Captain Harris stopped by with news. "We have more information about the men you're trailing. All five worked for over a year as security guards for different mines in the area. The man you killed in Shiprock seems to be the only one that left Denver. The surviving gang members have either quit their jobs or have been absent for at least three days."

"We believe the last three men are 'Big Bob' Stevens, Jim Gallahan and Alfredo Torrez." Handing Cody a piece of paper with the names on it, the captain continued, "I alerted the mines that there is a good possibility that these men were the ones responsible for all the gold shipment robberies. They'll do their own internal investigations to check this out."

"Wow! You sure discovered a lot of information captain. I really appreciate this."

"We're not sure that they're still in Denver, but my men have been alerted to look out for them so that we can bring them in for questioning."

"If I were them, I'd be thinking of taking my gold and skedaddling. They don't want me finding them again within the city limits."

"You've got a point there. I'll try and stop by with any further information," added Captain Harris as he left Cody's room.

The Denver police received word and passed it along to Cody that a body had been found on the trail a few days east of Denver that matched the description of Alfredo Torrez. It was now a week later, and Cody had begun to walk some around the hotel. His soreness was decreasing every day. Hopefully, he'd be close to normal in another week.

Captain Harris stopped by and gave Cody wanted posters that the Denver police had issued for "Big Bob" Stevens and Jim Gallahan. The posters stated that the pair were wanted for more than ten possible murders of mine guards and several gold thefts. A reward of $1,000 had been offered for each man dead or alive.

The captain added, "My men have checked all the hotels in Denver and these men are nowhere to be found. They were traced to a hotel about four blocks from here, but that was over a month ago. Of course, they could have been staying at one of the boarding houses since then. You know Cody, my employment offer still stands and it will remain open if you choose to accept it in the future. So, what are you planning to do?"

"I'm still waiting on the money transfer from Farmington and I need a little more time to fully recover from being shot. I figure it may be sometime late next week before I'm ready to leave."

True to his prediction, at the end of the next week Cody was feeling better and had received word that his money had arrived at the bank. He was now ready to leave Denver.

The night before he was to get back on the trail, Cody went to the front desk and asked if they had any stationery he could use. After he obtained a sheet of paper and an envelope, Cody headed back to his room to compose a letter to Tom.

Dear Tom,

I just wanted to drop you a note to let you know I'm doing okay. I'm in Denver now and a lot has happened during my trip. I was headed into the bank in Farmington to convert my gold into paper money when I ran smack into a bank robbery.

I had to shoot three robbers when one of them came after me. It turns out one of them was wanted and the sheriff paid me a $200 bounty to add to my cash roll.

I found one of dad's killers here and bested him in a gunfight. Unfortunately, he wasn't wanted, so I didn't earn a bounty. I also had a run-in with the three remaining gang members, but they got away. I believe that they have left Denver and I'm going to follow them. The Denver police chief told me one of them was found dead on the outskirts of town, so there are only two killers left to track down.

Please tell everyone hello, especially Jeb, and tell them not to worry. I'll try and send you another letter soon. I hope you are doing well.

Cody

When he checked out of the hotel, Cody didn't feel completely back to normal, but hoped he would be soon. Cody stopped at the bank to pick up his four hundred dollars, then mounted his horse and headed east out of Denver.

As he rode, Cody thought to himself, '*I wonder how long it's going to take me to find out where dad's killers went? I need to catch up to them quickly before they get too far ahead. Well, I guess it doesn't really matter. Hopefully, I'll have a long life ahead of me to find them and finish my quest.*'

THE END

PREVIEW – BOOK TWO

HANDS FASTER THAN LIGHTNING

AN UNCOMFORTABLE RIDE

"You don't have to die today," declared Cody.

"What makes you so sure that I'm the one that's gonna die?" asked Louis.

"Because everyone I've gone up against has died."

"I've been doing this for a lot longer than you, and no one has beaten me yet."

Louis Smith had been looking for Cody for three months. He'd just missed him in Shiprock and had been trying to catch him ever since. Louis was six feet tall and weighed one hundred seventy pounds. He had steely blue eyes, blonde shoulder-length hair and sported a mustache-beard combination on his long square face. Today he was wearing a white shirt and blue pants and had a right-handed gun belt and holster rig, slung low in the gunslinger style.

Cody was beginning to feel very nervous and his hands began to sweat. He'd never been sought out before, and it was a little creepy. His heart beat a tad faster. Cody thought, '*this guy might be faster than me since he's been doing this for a while.*' Cody tried to calm down some and take a few deep breaths. He remembered Tom's advice to watch the man's hands. "Well, there's always a first time, and I think it's going to be your last time."

"Confident, aren't you? Now the time has come to see which of us is the fastest."

"You can draw first."